"Please

Dani was begging—pleading with him to let her go. Because if she stayed, things would only get complicated.

"No." His voice was silky, holding her captive with that single word.

She caught her breath as he made a leisurely survey of her tautly held body. It occurred to her that he wasn't investigating new territory, but confirming what was already known.

With a satisfied nod he moved closer, coming to a stop where her legs sloped down off the hood of her car. Putting his hands on her knees, he drew them apart. She gasped when he insinuated his body firmly between her parted thighs. Her hands flew to his shoulders for balance, then stayed there out of sheer perversity.

"We *are* in a public parking lot," she protested breathlessly, wishing they weren't, astounded by his audacity, thrilled by his light touch. A frantic glance around the nearly empty lot revealed no inquisitive eyes. She didn't know whether to be relieved or alarmed.

Her body made its own decision. It was excited.

Emma Jane Spenser wrote this, her first Temptation, while her husband researched his doctorate at Oxford, and during her son's first years. After *A Novel Approach* was completed, the doctorate conveyed and the son turned four, she paused long enough to wonder how they'd done it all!

Then she and her family moved back home from England, only to pile into the car and start visiting. Somehow, while driving all over the country, Emma has continued to work on her second book. Eventually she'll be settling down in California, but will Emma be able to write without chaos around her? Stay tuned. . . .

A Novel Approach

EMMA JANE SPENSER

Harlequin Books

TORONTO • NEW YORK • LONDON
AMSTERDAM • PARIS • SYDNEY • HAMBURG
STOCKHOLM • ATHENS • TOKYO • MILAN

For Buster

FORTY YEARS OF
Romance

Published April 1989

ISBN 0-373-25348-6

1

THE WOMAN HIDDEN in the early-evening shadows watched the Corvette pull to an abrupt stop in front of the prestigious Denver restaurant. She'd first sighted the flashy car when it was nearly two full city blocks away, but then, it didn't take a keen eye to spot the metallic neon-orange paint that shrouded the sleek lines of the powerful sports car. Even from her comfortably distant post, the garish color was enough to make her cringe.

One of the uniformed men who staffed the parking facility moved to help the female passenger out of the car— a difficult feat considering the combination of her high heels and nearly prone position. The attendant struggled to place his hands at helpful but discreet locations on her body, and his obvious lack of success brought smiles to the faces of passersby. From her vantage point across the street, it was difficult to tell if the passenger was enjoying the experience or not. When the show was over, Dani transferred her attention to the driver.

He'd already jumped out of the car, and she watched as the slightly built man with the weasel face avoided tipping the valet by tossing his keys at the young man before hurrying to join his slinky companion under the brightly lit canopy. From this distance it was hard to fully appreciate the look on the valet's face, but Dani could easily imagine his frustration. Perhaps he'd do everyone a favor and lose the car.

Waiting only a moment, Dani checked the street for traffic before leaving the shadows to cross over to the restaurant. It would take a minute for the Weasel to check the woman's fur, then they'd be shown directly to their table. Although they were ten minutes late for their reservation, Dani was confident their table would be waiting. It was a weeknight, and while business wasn't slow, neither was it booming.

Timing was everything in this job, and Dani had calculated her own entrance down to the last second. The Weasel and his date would be concerned with their own comfort and wouldn't notice her arrival. Such details were important, particularly as she'd been following him around all week. Although she sincerely felt his powers of observation ranked with those of a mole in sunlight, she didn't want to take chances—not at this stage of the game. She was running out of time.

A gentle sigh of satisfaction escaped her lips when she saw the maître d' returning from seating the couple at a table located on a slight platform that ran along one side of the room. Dani congratulated herself, pleased that her telephone call had netted the desired results.

It was critical to her plan that they be seated at that precise table. Directly opposite the platform, separated by an expanse of scattered tables, was a bar. Not just a corner convenience, it lined one entire wall. The backdrop of glass and mirrors reflected the candlelight from the dining tables and added a glittering elegance to the already luxurious room. The polished wood of the bar itself basked under the loving attention of the bartender, and comfortable stools lined its length.

The players were in position now, and the adrenaline began to surge through her bloodstream. It would happen tonight.

Sticking closely to the script, Dani allowed her eyes to pan the length of the bar. Then she lifted her wrist to check the time on her watch and feigned mild irritation. Anyone watching the carefully orchestrated scene would deduce the obvious: some unfeeling lout was keeping this woman waiting.

Dani assured the maître d' that she would prefer to wait for her date at the bar rather than a table, then quickly walked forward before he could convince her to do otherwise. Strolling confidently on spike heels, Dani moved across the plush carpet to a nearby barstool. The fact that she chose the chair next to the place where the cocktail waitress filled her orders was no accident, and she stepped lightly onto the chair rung and sat down.

She knew she'd attracted a fair share of attention, particularly from the males in the room. That was okay. It was only the Weasel that she needed to avoid, and he was too busy trying to impress his companion to pay her any mind. In fact, Dani had deliberately worn one of the most sensuous dresses in her closet. The jade-green silk complemented her eyes as no other color could, and she had taken care to arrange her long thick blond curls in a deliberately loose and sexy style, with the heavy strands flowing down her back to her waist. After a week of disguises, it gave her a lot of pleasure to feel pretty for a change. And as long as the Weasel ignored her, it gave her added enjoyment to know she was no longer blending into the woodwork. While she normally didn't seek masculine admiration, a little silent appreciation from the males in the room gave her added confidence.

And tonight she needed every bit of confidence and courage she could summon.

Satisfied that her meticulous research had paid off, Dani gave her order to the bartender and relaxed against the cushions of her chair. A quick glance assured her that the scenario was absolutely perfect. From her perch at the bar she could look directly into the mirrored back-drop and keep an eye on the couple she'd been follow-ing.

Pulling out a few bills from the purse on her lap, Dani swept her gaze up and down the mirror. While she made a point of not staring at the table reflected directly in front of her, she kept its occupants in her peripheral vi-sion. It wouldn't do to have anyone notice her absorp-tion with the couple.

She gave the bartender a brief smile, paid for the drink he set before her and casually studied the rest of the room. An assortment of couples and larger parties took up nearly half of the tables. The stares she'd felt upon her arrival had dwindled to occasional glances, and she was pleased to see most of her admirers had returned their attention to their food and table companions. One man was eating alone, but he quickly averted his eyes when she looked in his direction.

Mindful not to remove her gloves, Dani cautiously sipped the Scotch she'd ordered. Though the delicate white lace gloves complemented the clinging sheath she'd worn, she felt a bit self-conscious about not removing them. But the simple precaution was necessary, and Dani firmly tamped down the uncomfortable thoughts. After all, she was the only one in the room who knew she kept them on to avoid leaving fingerprints.

Moments later the cocktail waitress appeared in the scene behind her, taking the Weasel's order. Dani had noticed on previous nights that the customers were given plenty of time to choose their drinks in order to tempt them with the appetizers that were listed on the leather-bound menu. Much to her surprise, it usually worked.

By the time the waitress arrived, most people had had several moments to appreciate the aromas surrounding them and needed immediate oral gratification in the form of expensive hors d'oeuvres.

Dani followed the girl's progress in the mirror, careful to stifle the sigh of relief when she didn't stop at another table. Additional orders would have brought disastrous consequences. Willing herself to relax, she sipped at her drink, allowing her gaze to drift over the rim as the waitress approached the work station.

The waitress gave the order for two drinks in the easy lingo of a true veteran of the bar. Dani nearly shouted with glee after loosely translating the order as Bourbon rocks and a Marguerita—easy to decide which drink belonged to the Weasel. The image he'd been trying to project all week was one of macho strength. No fruity concoction for this man.

As anticipated, the waitress moved away to perform other duties while the bartender filled the order and placed the glasses on the bar. He didn't linger, but went to serve another customer. Working quickly, Dani found the vial in her purse and uncapped it. Scanning the room, noting the location of the waitress, she took a deep breath. It was now or never. Absolutely no one was taking any notice of her.

Casually, she inched her hand over to the Bourbon and tipped the contents of the vial into the amber liquid. No sooner had she withdrawn her hand than the waitress returned, placed the drinks on her tray and headed back to the Weasel. With rapt attention Dani followed her progress in the mirror.

"Just what the blazes do you think you're doing?"

It wasn't a shout. It wasn't even a loud accusation, but the softly spoken words had the impact of bullets.

Dani's concentration shattered and she stared in wonder at the masculine hand that had appeared out of nowhere to capture her wrist. Looking up quickly from his hand to his face, Dani nevertheless took time to be impressed by the beautiful tailoring of the gray pinstripe which covered—but did not conceal—the solid torso beneath it. Solid and lethal. The understated power of a body held tightly in check seeped into the atmosphere surrounding them, causing her to momentarily forget her purpose. Blue eyes, icy with distrust and fired with something she couldn't quite identify, held her immobile and mute. And strangely excited. Goosebumps rose on her flesh, and she shivered in response to her unexpected reaction.

"Answer me, damn you! What did you put into that drink?" Still his words were discreetly quiet, at odds with the situation yet entirely effective.

Dani grimaced, not bothering to feign innocence. The tone of his voice told her everything. The jig was up. A solid week of planning and research had just been dumped in the garbage. She was stunned by the implications of his actions. She was furious. And, most surprising of all, she was very interested.

She concentrated on furious.

"If you had any idea how important this is to me, you'd mind your own business," she said forcefully, not unaware of the note of defiance in her tone. "I'll never get another chance like this!"

Adam stared disbelievingly into the flashing green eyes, his attention torn between the absurdity of the situation and his total awareness of the fragile wrist he still grasped. Just seconds ago he'd watched as the woman poured something into a drink—someone else's drink. One minute he was enjoying a quiet dinner and indulg-

ing in a particularly satisfying episode of people watching—the blonde in the green dress taking up all of his
attention—and the next thing he knew she'd done the
unthinkable. Reflexes made quick by training and
constant demand had propelled him across the room
to...what? He wasn't even sure anymore he'd seen what
he'd seen.

Adam shook his head as if to clear it, then refocused
on the woman he held captive. She wasn't watching him;
instead, her eyes were trained on the mirror. In that moment, he saw the reflection of the cocktail waitress and
the reality of the situation struck him. Someone was
about to be poisoned.

Releasing the woman, Adam sprinted over to the
raised platform, reaching the table just as the waitress
was leaving. The drink in question belonged to the man,
and Adam knocked it out of his fingers just as it was
being raised for that first sip.

"What the hell...?"

All eyes in the restaurant flew to Adam and the couple
at the table. Standing among bits and pieces of broken
glass, Adam breathed a sigh of relief. For whatever it was
worth, he'd just saved a life. Taking another deep breath,
he turned to confront the rapidly approaching maître d'.
Now there was time for the explanations.

But it wasn't going to be easy. He took a quick glance
at the bar, followed by a more careful search of the restaurant. Damn! The blonde was gone.

ADAM REREAD the lab results with total disbelief. Bourbon and water—or melted ice—was all it said. No cya-
nide. Not even a trace of arsenic. Just bourbon and water.

The suit he sported today was not much different from
the pinstripe of the previous evening. The quality, fit and

understated elegance were all the same, though the color was slightly different. It presented a solid, reliable air that was so vital to his business image. His clients were reassured by this carefully constructed front. It made their petitions for his help seem less tawdry, somehow less menacing. And considering what they were already suffering, Adam felt it was the least he could do to reassure them in this small way.

Last night he had caused an embarrassing scene at one of Denver's better restaurants. It had barely been worth the effort to try to explain. The customer was enraged, the maître d' appalled. The absence of the blonde had left him feeling—and looking—foolish and, Adam admitted, a bit disappointed.

He'd have liked to spend some more time watching the woman, even though her behavior had been highly suspect. But personal interest aside, he *had* seen her pour something into the drink, and he insisted on the contents being analyzed. While no one was even the slightest bit receptive to his explanation of an attempted poisoning, he was allowed to leave with the drink—or whatever he could scrape up from the floor.

Even the intended victim was singularly unimpressed by Adam's curt description of what he'd seen, and had a few choice words to say about the declining quality of clients at this establishment. All concerned were glad to see Adam, normally a valued customer, leave with unaccustomed haste. It was quietly agreed among the staff that perhaps he'd been working too hard and was in need of a rest.

To top it off, now the results of the analysis proved that Adam had been hallucinating. Or on a more positive note, perhaps the few fragments of glass he had supplied to the lab were inadequate for accurate testing.

And there was still the blonde. It would be difficult to conjure up a mirage quite as intriguing as the reality. Settling back comfortably in his desk chair, he let his mind wander back over the events of the previous evening.

Adam had been relaxing over an after-dinner drink, reveling in the peace and quiet of his own company, when the vision had entered the room. His attention had been riveted by her careless grace, absorbed by her every gesture. The luxurious mane of gold tresses cascaded about her shoulders, the heavy waves rippling gently every time she moved, flowing across her back and brushing intimately against the swell of her breasts.

She was a small woman, even in the stiletto heels she wore. Adam was just under six feet tall himself, and he figured that the top of her head would barely reach his chin. Barefoot, her nose would be somewhere around his chest.

A wave of sexual awareness washed over him as he envisioned a situation in which she would be standing near him, without any shoes, without any clothes. With a surprised start, he pulled his thoughts away from the highly erotic picture his mind had concocted and pursued his memories of the previous evening.

He had been content to watch her, taking care to avoid her eyes when she glanced around the room. It had been obvious she was meeting someone, and he'd fervently wished he could be that someone.

But then he'd watched as she emptied that vial, and everything had become confused. The flashing green eyes were now imprinted on his memory, a bonus from the moment when he'd confronted her. The clear, delicate features of her face weren't as readily called to mind, but he easily remembered her lips, parted in outrage at his interference, full and wet and enticing. Adam had nearly forgotten the reason behind their confrontation, but then she'd spoken, and her words had nudged him into action.

What exactly had she said? Something about how important this was to her?

The inter-office buzzer interrupted his thoughts, and he tossed the "bourbon and water" report aside. Acknowledging his secretary's warning that the driver was waiting to take him to the airport, he straightened his tie while lecturing himself sternly. It wasn't the end of the world, he'd have to just hope that no one besides the staff recognized him at that restaurant. With a muffled imprecation, he reminded himself that one of his favorite restaurants was now off-limits—unless he wanted to be constantly reminded of the scene he had caused.

Striding past the outer office, Adam calculated his chances of ever seeing the blonde again. Denver was big, but not *that* big, and he could improve the odds.

There were some things in life you just didn't leave to chance.

THE COFFEE Dani sipped no longer provided her with an adequate defense against the encroaching fatigue, but her reflexes brought the cup to her lips with automated regularity. Standing beside her desk, she once again reviewed the results of a full week's planning and coordination. She'd established the routine of the victim, and from this had devised a discreet and effective method of disposing of him. As a professional, she realized that even the best laid plans were subject to interference, but this time Dani was not amused.

Grimly she splashed the dregs of her coffee into a nearby plant. Not only had Pinhead—she'd dubbed him that in honor of his pin-striped suit and obvious lack of deductive reasoning—ruined an entire week's work, but now she was forced to come up with an alternate plan before another week was over.

She groaned at the twist the plot had taken, then reached to flip off the switch of the word processor before her temper caused her to hit the Erase key. She'd spent the entire night and nearly all of the morning hours wrestling with the calamitous events of the previous evening, and her bleary eyes were evidence of the long and aggravating struggle. What should have been the perfect murder had been greatly complicated by the unwelcome intrusion of an innocent bystander.

The aborted poisoning was now incorporated as part of the story, not because Dani enjoyed putting the scene down in words, but because it was just the sort of thing that would happen to a real murderer. It followed that the villain—aka Dani—would have to find another method for disposing of the victim. But she was running out of time! The completed manuscript was due to the publisher in just two weeks, and she couldn't bring herself to deviate from her unique method of ensuring that the plot was both realistic and plausible.

Dani's murder mysteries sold well, her latest having gained a respectable position on the *New York Times* Best Seller List. Writing under the pen name of Daniel Carmody, she pursued her career with a single-minded dedication that bordered on zealousness. She had determined early in her career that in order to make the crimes unique and believable, a simulated attempt upon an unsuspecting victim would be enacted. Dani figured that if she were able to perform the necessary steps and get away with murder, then the villain would likewise have similar luck. This logic had led her into some very embarrassing situations, the bungled job of the previous evening being a prime example.

She'd been the guest of the Denver police department on several occasions when a less-than-perfect plot had led to her detention. By now, however, they were growing used to her antics and normally let her out after an overnight stay—a token punishment that they kept hoping would curb her imagination.

The victims themselves were never quite sure what was happening and usually remained ignorant of their roles in the drama. They were never people she knew. Victim selection was quite arbitrary. She'd stroll through likely office buildings and malls until she happened upon a person—male or female—who happened to catch her fancy. Then she'd plan how to best dispose of her quarry. It was interesting work, and Dani loved every minute of it.

Although her family sometimes thought her sense of humor was a bit on the macabre side, Dani saw nothing unhealthy about her approach to writing. In her mind, she likened it to method acting.

And as far as the consequences went, she'd never been hauled into the station for attempted murder. It was always for something like disturbing the peace or loitering. Or even littering. Dani had once tried to throw a "bomb" into a parked car while driving her own truck past at an accelerated rate. And there was that vagrancy charge that still brought a smile to her lips....

Last night's poisoning—attempted poisoning, she corrected herself—was to have been the focus of her latest novel. Now she'd have to come up with something even more clever, thanks to Pinhead! Heading to the bedroom in the back of the house, Dani pulled off her jeans and top and replaced them with running shorts and a T-shirt, then sat down to pull on her shoes. Images of icy-blue eyes had been plaguing her all night, and her continual reference to "Pinhead" was the only way she could pull her wandering thoughts away from his admirable body and give his character the proper image of interfering busybody that he deserved.

Impatient with her thoughts, Dani let herself out of the house and, after a quick routine of warm-up stretches geared for runners, she fell into an easy rhythm that was designed to maximize her endurance and exercise her body without causing any damage. She had no time for any of the standard runner's ailments, and took great care to avoid injury. Running was necessary to her writing; it freed her mind and left her open to new ideas and plots. Without the repeated exposure to fresh air and exercise, Dani knew she wouldn't be able to produce the intricate mysteries that gave her such satisfaction.

Rounding the corner at the end of the block, she paused before crossing the street to the park on the other side. She'd chosen her home especially with this park in mind. Designed for walkers, runners and bikers, with separate areas and paths for each, it was ideal in the summer and fall. If you didn't mind soggy, muddy ground, it was also suitable in spring.

Dodging the occasional roller skater with an ease derived from years of practice, Dani tried to resurrect her earlier enthusiasm for the book. The plot was excitingly different from anything she'd done before. She had introduced political overtones to the basic mystery, a complicating factor that had taken more research—and more time! While she felt this book would stand out as her best work yet, there were moments when her original inspiration seemed altogether more trouble than it was worth. And now, just when she'd finally arrived at the point of executing the murder scenario, everything had started to fall apart.

Consequently, Dani was resentful toward the tall, dark-haired stranger who'd foiled her dastardly deed. Thanks to Pinhead, she had just a matter of days to plot, carry out and write yet another grisly scene. With an average dose of luck, the rest of the book would practically write itself, once the pivotal murder was nicely in place.

So why couldn't she get him out of her mind?

There was something about his eyes that tantalized her with wordless promises of exotic fantasies. The current that seemed to flow from his grasping fingers had merely captured her attention, but it was the eyes that had held her immobile. There had been something indefinable in his gaze that had left her totally adrift and confused.

She had felt wanted. And wanton.

In the light of day, Dani attributed her fantasies to an overactive imagination and the strain of the murder scenario. Blue eyes had never affected her before in such a fashion, and she refused to waste any more time analyzing her body's curious reaction to a perfect stranger.

She picked up the pace, her feet pounding a determined beat to the rhythm of Pinhead, Pinhead, Pinhead. . . .

IT SUITED ADAM'S PURPOSES to have the worst seat in the theater, particularly as he hadn't come to see the performance on the stage. Though a pillar neatly blocked most of the stage to the right of center, leaving him with a limited but clear view of the profiles of those actors who wandered over stage left, it wasn't the actors' profiles that interested him. It was the ebony-haired woman seated across the theater in a private box.

This was his first chance to observe her in person, and with the aid of the opera glasses he had rented for the evening, Adam studied her every expression. By the end of the first scene, he had noted and mentally catalogued each feature of her classically beautiful face.

Such knowledge was never useless, and he filed it away with the other details they had about the woman, never knowing which piece of the puzzle would provide the lever they needed. Their strategy was still in the formative stages, or as Chuck would say, "Watch and wait until something falls out."

But they didn't have the time to wait for some incriminating flaw to surface—one week, two at the most. If they didn't find the proof they needed by then, it would be too late.

After tonight Adam would be in a better position to observe the Channing woman. In fact, if everything went as planned, he would be sitting in her private box for the second act.

Focusing the glasses on the box, Adam took a final look at the people surrounding his subject. From the descriptions in the file, he knew they were all friends or acquaintances, but more important, none of them appeared to be her escort. She was in a party, not on a date, and that fell in nicely with his plans.

A movement from across the rows of seats caught his attention, and he deftly refocused to investigate. There was a slight stirring of the velvet drapes that covered the exit, and Adam figured someone was eager to hit the bar before intermission when the crowds would make it impossible. But before he could lower the glasses, the curtain moved again, parting just inches to reveal someone standing behind the heavy velvet. A glimmer of light reflected against a halo of upswept curls, and Adam experienced a rush of excitement in that first moment of recognition.

It was her . . . the blonde from the restaurant! Then, as he watched, she lifted a long, narrow object to her lips. It was much too long for a cigarette, but what else could it be?

Adam was on his feet and running down the aisle before he could consider his actions. Every second was critical. In just minutes intermission would begin and everything was set for him to "accidentally" meet Stephanie Channing and charm her into inviting him to join her party. That was no problem. At least, it wouldn't be a problem if he could take care of the blonde before then.

Exactly what he intended to do with her eluded him, but Adam shunted that thought aside. He'd worry about that later. Skirting the concession area, he slowed his pace to a fast walk, never once taking his eyes off the doorway where he'd seen her.

SOMEONE WAS SCREAMING, but it wasn't Dani.

She wanted to, but the large hand covering her mouth didn't permit even a squeak to pass her lips. Held tightly against her assailant's chest, she was effectively gagged and imprisoned: the full length cape she wore worked against her, hindering her attempts to kick her way free. Then, just as she was remembering the power of high heels against unprotected ankles, she was dragged away from the curtain and back out into the hall.

She could still hear the screaming, but it wasn't as loud.

"I'll take my hand away if you won't scream," a deep voice said.

Dani froze, her heart thumping madly. But the surprise was fleeting, and she eagerly nodded in agreement, more concerned with breathing than screaming. And between the pandemonium on stage and the thundering of her own heart, any additional noise she could produce would be feeble by comparison. Besides, Dani wasn't frightened enough to scream. Angry, perhaps. Frustrated, definitely. Especially because she hadn't even gotten off her first shot at the Weasel who was still sitting there—row T, seat 32—totally oblivious to the scene behind the curtain.

She wasn't frightened because, somehow, it didn't make sense to be frightened of the man she knew as Pinhead.

Cautiously the hand was removed. Dani did nothing to startle him, wishing she'd chosen a doorway that was closer to the center of activity rather than at the other end of a dim hallway. Away from prying eyes, she was completely at the mercy of a man who was probably very angry with her. Considering the likely outcome of the scene she had instigated in the restaurant, Dani suspected he intended to get even. But how had he found her?

"What's that thing in your hand?" he growled, then grabbed her wrist as he released her body from the encircling bonds of his arms. Plucking the straw from her fingers, he studied it from all angles, apparently mystified by the blue-and-yellow striped plastic tube.

"It's a straw," she said easily, hoping that he wouldn't ask what was in her other hand. No such luck. It might have been her expression of angelic innocence that kindled his suspicions, but moments later he had the corn kernels out of her palm.

With her weapon confiscated, Dani's next thought should have had something to do with escape. It didn't. The surprise she'd experienced at discovering *who* was holding her had given way to absolute delight at his thrilling touch. The adrenaline rush that had accompanied the windup to this second attempt to murder the Weasel was nothing compared to what she felt now.

"It's like I'm burning," she whispered, her lips caressing the words in wonderous astonishment. The excitement of their first meeting hadn't been an illusion; this fire inside of her was real, searing her with almost tangible flames.

"What did you say?" Jerking his attention away from the odd bits of 'evidence' in his hand, he narrowed his gaze on Dani.

Blushing furiously after saying those words aloud, Dani struggled to put a lid on her chaotic thoughts. Not one to indulge in emotional melodrama, she was feeling a bit silly. And, even though Pinhead was the unknowing catalyst of her discovery, it didn't have anything to do with him. Not really. After all, he was a stranger, not to mention a source of considerable irritation. Without much effort on his part, he was already sabotaging her career. She certainly didn't need him doing that to her heart!

As if that were possible, Dani reminded herself. Attraction was miles away from love and light-years from trust, and that was a road she never intended to travel again.

"If I'd wanted you to hear, I would have said it louder," Dani said smartly, wishing her comeback could be more scathing. But she was too busy planning her escape to be able to spare much thought for spirited repartee.

An annoyed shake of his head was his initial response, but his subsequent question told Dani in no uncertain terms that it was time she vacated the premises. "What are you doing with a peashooter?" he demanded, the glimmer of suspicion expanding when he saw her flinch.

"None of your business." Dani's hopes for a quick getaway collapsed when she saw his brows rise at her sassy reply.

"I can make it my business," he returned smoothly, levering her closer with a sudden flex of his fingers on her wrist. Dani was sure he intended the move to be menacing, but waving the inoffensive straw in her face spoiled the end result. Nevertheless, standing that close, almost touching him, Dani perceived that the situation was rapidly disintegrating.

"It's not a peashooter. It's a straw." She'd decided against buying a peashooter. It would have been easier for the cops to trace than the straw. And since she'd planned on leaving the weapon at the scene of the crime, that was an important consideration.

"You used it like a peashooter," he insisted.

"No, I didn't." Not yet, anyway. Besides, in Dani's mind, it was more of a blowgun than a peashooter, just like the corn kernels were really poisoned darts. She sighed. So much for yet another brilliant murder scenario. And just who *was* this guy? The Weasel's bodyguard?

"I don't know what you're up to," he said, "but you're not getting away with it this time." Cool eyes regarded her steadily, letting her know who was in charge.

He wasn't bluffing, she realized. Somehow, he was convinced he'd thwarted a real criminal. Well, almost convinced, she corrected as he flicked another glance at the straw and corn. He just wasn't sure how big a crime she might be committing. Dani decided to use that uncertainty to her own advantage.

"Don't be too sure," she challenged. "How do you know I haven't already succeeded?"

"What?" His eyes flew back to her small armory, disbelief registering in his expression. "Who?" he asked. Then, even more bewildered, "How?"

Dani nearly laughed, but caught the impulse in time. He only needed one more push. Indicating the theater, she said, "The guy who looks like he's sleeping." Then she pasted a bland expression on her face, daring him to call her bluff.

It worked.

Visibly disturbed by her outrageous claim, he appeared oblivious to the thunder of applause signaling the end of the first act. Dragging Dani along behind him, he pulled open the door to the seating area.

"Sorry, but I gotta go." The apology prefaced Dani's next move, which was to dig her heel into the toe of his shoe. His bellow of outrage coincided with the outward flow of people from the theater, and he was startled into releasing her wrist.

Even then, Dani's escape would have been temporary if it weren't for the tall balding man who latched on to his arm as he turned to give chase.

"Hey, Winters! It's now or never if you want to meet Stephanie."

Her cape billowing out behind her, Dani tore down the hall and plunged through the exit, silently blessing . . . and envying . . . a woman named Stephanie.

2

DANI PULLED HERSELF OUT of the water and carefully made her way across the slick wet tiles to where she'd left her carryall. She tugged off the bathing cap and shook free the slightly damp locks of hair, gratified when her scalp was no longer smothered under rubber. She didn't need her disguise anymore, because her victim was already out of sight, in the Jacuzzi room. The club was nearly empty now, and the pool area itself was deserted. Although it was still relatively early in the evening, most of the members had better things to do on a Saturday night than pump iron and swim laps.

That is, everyone except Dani and the Weasel.

The health club was her—and *his*—last chance. If he survived this third attempt, Dani didn't think she would have the heart to try again.

For the past several nights, she had watched as the Weasel walked the eight blocks to the health club where he went through the motions of an exercise program. From what she'd been able to observe, the weights he lifted did not appear too demanding, and the laps he swam could be counted on one hand. The majority of his time at the club was spent in the whirlpool.

This was where Dani planned to kill him. She just hoped he stayed put long enough to allow her to do it. Most evenings, after his joke exercise program, he'd either persuade a young lady to accompany him for dinner, or if unsuccessful, he'd go on the prowl through various singles clubs.

More often than not, though, he was successful. It wasn't his looks and greasy charm that attracted the young women, Dani knew. It was his talk. Talk of money. How much he had. How much he planned to have. And what he intended to do with quite a bit of it that night.

For her own part she'd been forced to keep to the shadows, always alert to the threat of his roving eye. That was the real reason the Weasel came to this particular club. Normally filled to the brim with young, well-built men and women, it was a particularly good spot for a bit of body watching. And if any of the young women happened to catch his interest, the Weasel was not shy about introducing himself.

The last thing Dani needed was to attract his attention, so throughout the surveillance period she'd kept a swimming cap over her blonde hair, a knee-length, terry cloth robe around her petite curves, and a pair of clear-lens glasses across her nose. Her less-than-attractive disguise kept her immune to the Weasel's roving eye while she'd mapped out his routine and plotted her own course of action.

The planning for the poisoning attempt had been much easier, and even the attack at the theater had been straightforward. Now the only place outside of his apartment or office that he frequented with any regularity was this club.

Tonight was the night for the murder. With the facility nearly deserted, Dani knew she'd never have a better chance. The Weasel was alone in the whirlpool, and she knew he'd soon leave if no one arrived to keep him company. With an eye on the closed door of the Jacuzzi room, she quickly unzipped the bag and retrieved the sign and masking tape. It was time to take precautionary measures against interfering busybodies. On bare feet, she swiftly crossed the tiles to the frosted glass door and efficiently taped the Out of Order sign at eye level.

Satisfied that the Weasel would now be assured of total privacy, she retrieved her belongings and rounded a nearby corner. A quick look at the deserted hallway assured her that she was not being observed, and she knelt on the floor beside an electrical outlet.

She'd already measured the distance from the outlet to the whirlpool, and the cord she removed from her bag was just a few feet longer than was necessary, giving her a margin for error. She was sweating now as she taped one end of the cord to the electrical outlet. Leaving her bag in place, she then proceeded to unwind the cord from its neat loops, laying a path around the corner to the Jacuzzi room.

Taking a deep breath, she opened the door and threw the remaining length of rope into the pool where it landed with a plop between the startled Weasel and . . . another man.

The Weasel just looked at her curiously, screwing up his features as though trying to remember where he'd seen that face. But Dani gave him no thought; all her attention was focused on the unexpected witness/victim at the other end of the bubbling pool.

Blue eyes traced the length of cord to the spot where Dani stood frozen. She stood mesmerized as his gaze traveled up her bare legs, pausing at the swell of her breasts and finally breaking away to reach her face. There was recognition in those eyes, and Dani was at the same time delighted and appalled.

Delighted that he remembered. Appalled that he remembered. With one half of her concentration she willed
herself to remain calm and collected under his very
thorough study of her body, wishing that she'd pulled on
the robe over her one-piece bathing suit. The thin mail-
lot was cut high over her smooth thighs and dipped low
in the back. She would have to remember not to turn
away. There was only so much scrutiny she could stand.

With the other part of her concentration, she studied
the body that was only half covered by the bubbling
water of the pool.

Pinhead. How could she ever have given this man such
a misnomer! Interfering, he was. A busybody, maybe.
But other, more appropriate nicknames flitted through
her mind. Like Gorgeous George. Handsome Harry.
Sensuous Sam. Or just plain Adonis. From what she
could see above the water line, the combination of hard
muscles and smooth, sleek skin lived up to what she'd
imagined was under the pin-striped suit that night at the
restaurant. Forgetting for the moment that she was here
on a mission of murder, Dani allowed herself the self-
indulgence of staring.

The thrill of seeing his green-eyed illusion surged
through Adam. She was back. And she was doing
something quite bizarre, again. Not alarmed in the least
by her actions, he controlled his features and vowed to
get some answers. At the very least, he wanted her name.
The frankly approving gaze in her eyes as she dissected
every inch of his body that she could see above water
gave him hope.

"What are you doing?" he asked in a low, evenly
pitched voice. He was leaning casually against the side
of the pool, a mere ten feet away. His eyes never left hers,

not even to further examine what she'd thrown into the water.

For a split second Dani wondered if he wanted to know why she was staring. But meeting his eyes, she realized he didn't have to ask that particular question. He knew! She flushed, all the way to her toes, then fixed her gaze on his nose as she answered his real question.

"Electrocuting the Weasel." Well, he *had* asked, and the truth just rolled off her tongue.

Adam let his eyes fall on the other man in the pool, then nodded his understanding.

"What weasel?" The scratchy tenor of her victim's voice grated on her nerves. Dani thought he must be incredibly stupid not to recognize a murder attempt when he saw one. But no matter, he was finally dead now. He'd just been electrocuted.

Along with Adonis. Whoops.

Dani grimaced, not enjoying the realization of how this new development would further scramble the plot of her book. She was famous for well-planned, well-executed murders, not the messy half-witted eliminations she'd performed lately. But she comforted herself with the knowledge that this time she had been successful at least.

Neither Adam nor Dani bothered to answer the Weasel.

Adam reached forward to grasp the cord, then studied it carefully. Flicking the frayed end of the hemp rope against one palm, he asked casually. "Any particular reason?"

She got angry, then, and her words were full of righteous indignation. "This room was marked Out of Order."

Adam looked past Dani to the door. A square of paper lay face down on the tiles. "Masking tape doesn't stick well to a surface covered with condensation," he said with just a trace of reproach in his voice.

Dani followed his gaze with her own, then briefly shut her eyes in frustration. But she quickly flicked open the lids; it wouldn't do to let her guard down around Pinhead.

"Now I'll have to think of something else," Dani huffed. Privately she was tempted to let things stand and allow Adonis to die along with the intended victim. He surely deserved that, or worse, for all his interference. But the outline didn't account for an extra body.

Still, her author's mind rolled over the possibilities. The editor would go along with a relatively minor change in plot. That is, as long as the book was completed on time.

Dani postponed deciding between the double murder and toiling on the word processor to describe this third botched attempt, then formulating another murder scenario. She'd never created such an inept villain. Dani wondered if she was losing her touch.

"Think of something else for what?" The Weasel was getting curious, and this served to irritate Dani all the more. A dead victim would definitely be more palatable at this point, but she rarely let the victims influence their own part in the fiction. If she decided against the double electrocution, it would now be extremely difficult to plan and carry out yet another attempt at what should have been a simple, cut-and-dried murder. There was nothing more annoying than an alerted victim.

"Yes," Pinhead drawled, "please tell us."

She was rapidly being swayed to the side of the double murder. But the husky voice cut into her thought processes and brought her back to the present. It was time for her disappearing act. She unglued her eyes from their study of a certain pinhead's sensuous lips, then turned and bolted through the open door before either man could react.

"Hey, wait a min—" The Weasel was cut off before he could finish, startled by Adam's sudden pursuit. He stared open-mouthed as Adam threw himself across the narrow expanse of water and vaulted out of the pool. Then he, too, disappeared into the larger room beyond the Jacuzzi, leaving the Weasel alone in the bubbling pool with the soggy rope for company.

Moments later the frayed rope slithered noiselessly out the door.

EVEN THOUGH he was only seconds behind the fleeing blonde, Adam still managed to lose her. Pulling himself to an abrupt halt, he surveyed the empty area carefully. The Olympic-size pool was empty, as were all the chairs and lounges. Satisfied that his quarry was not in the pool room, he took the most logical step. He followed the rope from the Jacuzzi room, around the corner and into the hallway. With a sense of true accomplishment, his eyes lit upon the abandoned carryall. Bending down, he studied the electrical socket with its attachments of tape and rope.

Rope did not conduct electricity. Likewise, Bourbon and water did not poison. For that matter, straws and corn kernels didn't . . . Well, didn't what? He still wasn't sure of that one. Adam had always prided himself on his ability to use logic to arrive at a reasonable solution to most any problem. After all, it was his business to routinely solve complicated puzzles. And now, his conclusion was quite obvious. The green-eyed blonde was trying to kill someone without killing them.

He grinned at his deductions, without trying to pursue the puzzle further. There were any number of motives for her behavior, and it would be a waste of his time to try to fathom them. What he really wanted was the woman. If she chose to explain her actions, fine. He didn't care. That wasn't the reason he wanted her.

He pulled the end of the rope away from its moorings, then slowly wound the full length into a neat pile at his feet, one end slithering down the hall trailing a bit of water. Carefully he stored the rope in the carryall, then picked it up and proceeded to the men's locker room. There he showered and changed into street clothes, taking care not to hurry.

She'd wait for him. He'd found her car keys in the bag.

ADAM LOCATED the car easily. It was the only one in the parking lot that had a green-eyed blonde sitting on the hood.

"You certainly took your time," she said, her eyes not quite meeting his as he strolled across the asphalt.

"I figured you'd wait."

The timing was off, Dani worried. He was too distracting, on two fronts. One as Pinhead; the other as Adonis. His blue eyes flashed a signal of unmasked interest, and she determinedly tried to tamp down the fires flickering deep inside. It had been a lot of years since Greg, she thought abstractedly, but even then she couldn't remember feeling like this when they were together. She was burning up inside, a sensation as alien to her as it was exciting.

She wasn't ready for this, not the interference, and especially not the man himself. The excitement he generated was too new, and Dani was confused by her reaction to it.

Her book was her first priority. She had to concentrate on the book. Dani forced her gaze away from the hypnotizing blue orbs and frantically drew one deep breath, then another. The calming effect was negligible, but it was enough to allow Dani to superficially compose herself.

"I need my keys." She held out her hand.

He ignored it. Adam dropped both bags, his and hers, to the pavement beside his feet.

She decided to change the subject. "I don't believe in coincidence." The extra-long time he'd taken in the locker room had given Dani more than ample time to dwell on his appearance here at the health club, not to mention the theater. And she hadn't come up with any answers. How could he possibly have known where to find her?

"Neither do I." Adam decided not to explain yet. He'd rather keep her off balance, at least until he was in possession of the information he wanted, such as who she was, and where she lived and if he had any serious competition.

"Please give me my keys." She was begging, pleading with him to let her go, to return her keys; because if she stayed, things would only get complicated. On both fronts.

"No." He denied her request in a silky voice and held her captive with a single word.

Dani caught her breath as his eyes performed a leisurely survey of her tautly held body, alert to the slight nod of his head as she expelled the air in a quick whoosh. It occurred to her he wasn't investigating new territory, but confirming what was already known. Another satisfied nod, and his eyes returned to capture hers.

He excited her more with his eyes than any man had ever done with kisses. She wanted him, and she was shocked with that wanting. At no time in her life had she experienced such instant attraction. She conveniently forgot the fruitless hours she'd spent this last week trying to erase his persistent image from her memory. Now she realized she had only succeeded in banishing Pinhead, the busybody. No nicknames, no simple categories...standing before her with a man, a very formidable man! Someone infinitely more dangerous than Pinhead and Adonis because he was real.

At any other time, the thin cotton shirt she wore would have felt adequately modest. But today, Dani was aware that nothing could possibly hide her body's reactions from this man's gaze. Her breasts began to swell with the heat that surged with increasing speed through her veins. The delicate tips hardened into unmistakable buds of anticipation, pushing against the rough cotton. But whether or not he could actually see the changes her body was experiencing made no difference; Dani knew he could read the signals it was sending without the more obvious clues.

She sat very still as he moved closer, coming to a stop where her legs sloped down off the hood. She was wearing slacks, and he put his hands on her knees, drawing them apart. Dani gasped when he insinuated his body firmly between her parted thighs. Her hands flew to his shoulders for balance, then stayed there out of sheer perversity.

"We *are* in a public parking lot," she protested breathlessly, wishing they weren't, astounded by his audacity, thrilled by his light touch. A frantic glance around the nearly empty lot revealed no inquisitive eyes. She didn't know whether to be relieved or alarmed. Her body made its own decision; it was excited.

She felt good, he thought. Even better than he'd expected, but then, he'd spent a week anticipating this. Her welcoming softness was not a surprise, rather a confirmation of every instinct he possessed. He'd known she would be perfect, that they would meld into an unforgettable union. Even through the barrier of clothing, Adam knew. The disparity of their sizes made no difference. The fact that they knew nothing about each other was unimportant. They belonged together.

The part of him that was undeniably masculine nestled more intimately against her, and he closed his eyes briefly as he reveled in the exquisite pleasure coursing through his body. A moment, no more, then he raised his lids to capture her stunned reaction.

Her lips were parted, glistening from the recent caress of her tongue. Adam didn't need a clearer invitation. But as he began to lower his mouth to hers, his fingers caught a swift hint of tension from where they still rested on her thighs, a tension that had nothing to do with sexual anticipation. He halted his approach to analyze. It was important that he didn't make any mistakes, at least not any critical ones. This time it was for keeps. The kiss could wait.

Dani remained tense against the warmth of his hands, the intimacy of his thighs. The part of her that had avoided sexual relationships for so many years had responded automatically, reminding her of the humiliation she'd suffered before. But, for the first time, the memory was vague, not sharply painful. Nonetheless, it was still there.

"No." She forced out the word, more a plea than a command, wondering why she'd bothered when he already appeared to have changed his mind. And with that realization, Dani felt the heat of a true, girlish blush climb over her. A bit late to be saying no, she thought, overwhelmingly conscious of the hard warmth snuggled between her thighs. Skipping over embarrassment—she'd allow herself that luxury in private—she went directly to the offensive.

"No!" She amended her tone, determined to call finito to this ludicrous scene. Glaring into the curious eyes above her, she crossed her arms defiantly under her breasts, a movement which drew his gaze to the still excited nipples beneath her shirt.

"Of course not," he agreed smoothly. He had no intention of arguing. More battles were won with subtlety and tactics than with outright confrontation. Adam regretfully took a step backwards, pushing her legs closed before thrusting his hands into his back pockets. The denim of his faded jeans stretched tightly across his hips, emphasizing that hardness which Dani was trying so desperately to ignore.

"Give me my keys." She tried to make her voice firm, to cover up the trembling. If she could get away, maybe she could pretend nothing had happened, that she hadn't allowed a total stranger to come so close. That she hadn't responded to a blatantly sexual overture from a man she didn't even know.

And she could make herself believe that she didn't want him to touch her again.

"Where do you live?" He asked the question as if he had every right to the answer. Maybe he did, she mused, then pushed that thought aside. She was imagining things.

"I don't have time for you now." Dani didn't bother to employ the normal feminine evasions of the impropriety of the situation. After all, he'd witnessed three murder attempts—no, make that witnessed two and died in the third. And he'd effected a unique assault on her body that left her in no doubt as to his desires.

She didn't even attempt to protest that they were strangers. She felt as if she'd known him forever. Or wished she had.

"We'll make time."

"No."

"Yes."

The old memories of deceit and rejection that had governed her existence for countless years were fading rapidly in the face of his determination. The sudden absence of loneliness was as astonishing as was her need to allow him to make such drastic changes in her life. Dani knew he wasn't even aware of what he was asking of her.

She wasn't going to make it easy for him.

"Give me my keys or I'll scream."

Looking at her without surprise, Adam figured he'd pushed about as far as he could today. She needed room to breathe, to think. He was confident enough to give her both.

He prayed he was right.

"You should have used that line ten minutes ago."

"Better late than never," she said, then held out her hand. She was startled, and a bit disappointed, when he fished her keys out of a back pocket and dropped them onto her open palm.

She slid off the hood, then pushed the key into the lock. She was lucky; her shaking hands were shielded from his gaze by her body. When Dani opened the door, she turned to find her carryall thrust into her arms. But he didn't immediately let go.

"My name is Adam Winters. I've lived here in Denver all my life and run a profitable business. I'm not married, have never been married and have no children that I'm aware of."

Adam Winters. Dani liked it, even better than Adonis.

He paused, watching to see if any of this made any difference. He couldn't tell, so he decided to finish with it. Maybe something he said would take away the fears that were making her run now. "I want to see you again. Not just once."

"I know." It was useless to pretend otherwise. They both knew she wanted the same.

"I'd also be interested in hearing about the Weasel."

That woke Dani up from what amounted to a trance. Dropping the bag into the passenger seat, she planted herself firmly behind the wheel, then looked up at the man leaning into the car through the open door.

"I can't tell you." That was one of the rules. She couldn't make the game easier by enlisting aid. Her murderers counted on total secrecy.

"Never?" Adam didn't think he could stand not knowing. Besides, it gave him a firm link to the woman behind the crimes.

"I . . . don't know." Dani was getting confused between the reality of Adam and the fantasy of killing the Weasel. Or was Adam the fantasy? "I'll tell you after I decide whether or not he's dead."

Adam nodded as if he understood her answer, then closed the door of her car, stepping away to pick up his bag. He was still in her rearview mirror as she pulled into the southbound lane of traffic.

She knew she'd see him again. The thought cheered her immensely.

3

THERE WASN'T ANY WAY around it. He was going to have to stay dead. They both were.

Dani had spent yet another sleepless night confronting her plot dilemma. She'd wasted the first half of the evening struggling to keep Adam alive, then had given in to temptation and let him rest in peace, right alongside the Weasel. The second half of the night and the early hours of the morning were given over to committing her final decision to paper—or, technically, to word processor. Now the sun was gaining height on the eastern horizon and she took her fingers off the keys for the first time in hours.

The deed was done. And as much as Dani disliked admitting it, the entirely new plot, which was an unavoidable consequence of the accidental death of an innocent bystander, had resulted in a very credible story-line.

Dani spent another few moments mulling over the complicated plot twist, then reached for the phone beside her terminal. She'd already sold her original outline to the publisher, but the murder mystery she was in the process of writing bore only a vague resemblance to her earlier proposal. She'd better let her agent in on the change now. Although Dani still had a week before the manuscript was due, Agnes would need that time to convince the publisher that this Daniel Carmody murder mystery was up to standard, perhaps even a brilliant addition to the long line of best-selling novels. Either way, Dani wasn't worried.

Perhaps next year she'd give the original plot another try, assuming a certain man wasn't around to interfere. The thought didn't give her any pleasure.

Agnes Millhouse had been Dani's agent since the beginning, just as Dani had been her first client, but their relationship hadn't started there. Rather, it had begun the first year of college when the two girls had shared a room. The agent-author collaboration had been something of an accident. Upon graduation, Dani had expressed an intention to write a book. Agnes bet her that if she finished the book, she could figure out a way to sell it. Now, six years later, Dani was a successful author and Agnes was a successful agent.

They were also still close friends. Fortunately for Dani, Agnes kept that in mind when Dani called at the crack of dawn.

"Plot change, Dani? You don't have time for a plot change." Dani smiled at the panic in Agnes's voice. Teasing her friend was a favorite pastime.

"I ran into some trouble with the poisoning a while back, and had to ad lib another scenario. And a few other things." Dani didn't think details were important at this time. Agnes could read it all next week when she got the completed manuscript. True to detail, Dani had left out nothing. Well, almost nothing. The scene in the parking lot had happened after Adam was already dead.

"Did you find someone else to put up the bail?" Jumping to the conclusion that Dani was in jail was a conditioned response from Agnes. She wasn't always mistaken.

"No, nothing like that." Dani was hesitant, not wanting to share the gory details of her plot reversals. Even

as confident as she was that the new story was as good—
or better—than anything she'd written before, she was
loath to defend her uncharacteristic fumbling. "It's just
that some bystander interfered. Twice. And I finally
killed him."

"Did he know?" Agnes was always able to follow
Dani's unorthodox train of thought. She'd had plenty of
practice.

"Kind of." Adam had known she was trying to murder the Weasel; she'd told him that much. Simple logic
would point out that he, too, was now a victim.

"No. Nothing like that," she said for the second time.

"Are you going to be late then?" Agnes pressed.

"Oh, no!" Dani had never missed a deadline before,
and this morning she'd been relieved to know that she'd
not miss this one. The rest of the book would practically
write itself now. All she needed was a week of peace and
quiet. Luckily her first draft usually closely resembled
her last, requiring only a few last-minute grammar and
spelling changes.

"Not to worry, Agnes," she reassured the agent. "I just
wanted to warn you about the changes."

"Can you give me a new outline or summary?"

"Sorry, Agnes," Dani said, fielding the request. "Not
and still finish on time. Besides, the changes are more to
do with the characters. The basic plot still . . . well, it re-
sembles the original one. Kind of." She had no intention
of wasting her precious time with a summary when the
manuscript would soon be done. "You can tell them I
think it's good. In fact," she said with growing confidence, "if nothing else goes wrong, I think it will be one
of my best."

"They're all your best." Agnes sounded as though she
had decided to forgive her for the initial panic.

"Thanks, Agnes." Dani grinned, now knowing why she had called her friend. Just talking with Agnes restored her confidence in her writing. Agnes's common-sense approach to their parallel careers encouraged a balance that Dani relied upon, especially when things weren't going as planned.

"Now get back to work," Agnes ordered. "I'll see you next Tuesday." It was a tradition for Dani to hand over the typed manuscript over lunch at a terribly expensive local restaurant, and the date had been on her calendar for months. With luck, they wouldn't have to cancel.

Dani hung up the phone and flipped off the computer. She was going to ignore Agnes's instructions, at least for the time being. It was time for rest, not work. Anyway, it was quieter at night. She did her best work then, the dark shadows lending a sinister influence to her writing. Now, in the light of day, she'd seclude herself in the comfort of her hideaway and laze away the day. A few hours' sleep, a fancy meal prepared with loving care and then another nap would have her energized for the night ahead. She had nearly a quarter of the book left to write, she realized with a slight pang of nervousness, then scoffed at her temporary loss of confidence. She'd done it before. When the ideas were there, when the plot was firm in her mind and the characters solidly planned, then all she had to do was sit and let her fingers fly over the keyboard.

And this book was turning out to be easier than most . . . to write, that is, not to plan. Never had she become so involved with her characters. In fact, the hint of humor that was seeping into the novel was both entertaining and exciting. Her inept villain was, surprisingly, a joy to work with, and the victim waltzed through the early part of the story in unknowing bliss. The plot involving the second—unplanned—victim was an enigma that would take the reader on a merry ride, even after his death.

Dani couldn't wait to get back to work.

But she contained her enthusiasm and went through the motions of securing the house. Checking to see that the downstairs doors were locked, she flipped off the lights as she made her way through the house and headed up the stairs.

There was a single door at the top of the staircase, and this was kept closed all the time Dani was in the house. It was the dividing point between her private life and her work. Downstairs was a small bedroom that she used for catnaps when she was on a marathon writing spree. She also kept her running clothes there so she could step away from the computer at any time and be outside in the fresh air within minutes. A small bathroom served the same convenience.

A tidy living room, just off the front door, was reserved for those acquaintances who were not friends, salesmen who deserved a few minutes of her time, dates who must be invited to sit somewhere if she was running late, and the miscellaneous visitors that one had to cope with while living in a large city.

The largest room on the ground floor was her office. It was furnished thoughtfully, with all the comforts and necessities at her fingertips. To counteract the "indoors" quality of the room, a lavish assortment of plants and small trees decorated every available surface.

This vegetation brought its own demands on her time. As natural light in the room was limited to a small window, Dani was forced to rotate the plants twice weekly with others throughout the house. It was a chore that she didn't enjoy, but a necessary one. And while her cleaning lady, Myra, would not dream of taking on the additional work—"I don't feed animals or lug around plants," she'd said when Dani had hired her years earlier—they were able to work out a compromise—Myra's muscle-bound son would come over and shift the green stuff when Dani was out of town, leaving Dani to fend for herself when she was in residence.

All in all, the downstairs was a utilitarian living and working space. Dani had been careful to design it so that it appeared complete. Anyone walking in to the house would assume it was the primary living space.

They would be wrong.

Upstairs, behind a closed door, was Dani's real home. Only close friends and family were even aware of its existence. It was there that Dani headed now, the downstairs carefully secured so she might enjoy her solitude with no worries of interruption.

She put her hand on the doorknob and slowly turned it. It always gave her pleasure to come up here, particularly after a grueling session at the computer. Taking a deep cleansing breath she allowed the feeling of well-being to surface as she pushed the door shut behind her. She stood there, taking pleasure in the scene before her.

The room, if you could call it that, took up the entire second floor of the house. Windows, some floor to ceiling, some smaller, stretched in a nearly unbroken pattern around the entire area. They gave the room a bright, almost open sensation—so different from her office below. There were billowing French drop curtains fixed to each window, but during the daylight hours, Dani rarely used them.

To the right of the door was what she called the living room. Set upon a slight platform, was a mass of soft, deeply cushioned furniture complemented by dozens of small and large pillows that were scattered on, around and beside the sofas and chairs.

On her left was the bedroom, another raised platform supporting miscellaneous bedroom furniture, including cherrywood bedside tables, wardrobes and a dresser. But they were all dwarfed by an enormous bed. Dani was a restless sleeper, and the bed was more a necessity than a luxury. After rolling off her single bed countless times over the years, she found the security and logic of a bigger bed were unavoidable. The rose-hued counterpane of the bed blended delicately with the smoke-blue carpet and striped silk easy chairs.

The only solid partitions in the room housed the bathroom. Dani had plenty of space to utilize, so she'd not skimped in alloting this room its due share. The shower, glassed in on three sides and the fourth a slab of polished marble, was big enough for a small crowd. Its size was a necessity, her plants needed regular baths.

Back in the very center of the room, surrounded by a highly polished wood floor, was what she'd dubbed her activity area. In function, it was a kitchen. Cooking was Dani's passion, a pastime which made exercise mandatory.

There was a terrific equilibrium in her life that Dani felt was epitomized by the kitchen at the center of her living space. Cooking was a normal activity, while writing was slightly beyond the average scope. Her efforts in the kitchen restored normalcy to an otherwise erratic lifestyle.

Attempting to look at the room through the eyes of a stranger, Dani wondered how Adam would like it. It wasn't even a question of *if* he'd ever see the room. She'd known when she drove away from the parking lot that Adam was only letting her go temporarily, that it suited him to let her run away. He'd soon invade her home. It was only a matter of time. He'd already invaded her thoughts.

She didn't trouble herself with thoughts of *when* she'd see him again. The details she'd leave up to Adam. She had enough to be responsible for without taking on unnecessary worries. It would require some imagination to find her—particularly as there were a lot of things he didn't know. Her name, for starters. And where she lived.

She moved wearily to the bed, stripping off her clothes as she crossed the thick carpet, leaving them draped carelessly on the easy chair as she passed. She pulled back all the coverings piling them at the foot of the massive bed until only a crisp sheet was left to cover her aching body, then climbed in and rested her head on a small mountain of feather pillows. She was asleep in seconds.

ADAM WAS CERTAIN he wanted to see her again. But he wasn't concerned about the minor details. He already knew where she lived. And, of course, he knew her name.

Danielle Courtland.

There were other assorted facts, such as her age. Danielle was twenty-eight as of her last birthday, and Adam couldn't have been more pleased. Although it wouldn't have made any difference to his plans, the smaller the age gap, the easier it would be to merge their lives. It was a pleasant surprise to discover he was just eight years her senior.

He also had a copy of her police record. That didn't worry him, not really.

True, her rap sheet was relatively innocent, compared to those he was used to reading. But hers was certainly the most interesting he'd ever read. No convictions, not even any prosecutions. And the charges, all of which had been dropped within hours or days of their initial recording, were a fascinating collection of the most minor offences mixed with the ludicrous. Littering and soliciting? Trespassing and disturbing the peace? Operating an unauthorized vehicle in a pedestrian area? His personal favorite was vagrancy. He couldn't wait to hear the story behind that one.

It didn't occur to Adam to take any of the charges at face value. After all, he'd personally witnessed—or thought he had witnessed—Danielle doing some very bizarre things, and was convinced a less tolerant person might interpret her actions in a fairly sinister manner. Thus the rap sheet.

Discovering her name and address had been a fairly routine matter. At least, it was routine for a private investigator, and that happened to be what he was. Although he normally specialized in cases of blackmail and embezzlement, he could still find a "missing person" when pressed. Danielle had been correct; meeting her at the health center had not been a coincidence.

He would have found her sooner if he hadn't had to spend two full days testifying in New York. And this was one case he wasn't assigning to any of his operatives.

He'd taken the Weasel's name and address the night Adam had "saved" his life at the restaurant. Logic had told him that by sticking close to the Weasel, he would eventually run in to the blonde again.

Later, although it hadn't been easy to let her drive away, Adam had been confident that he'd be seeing her again very soon. A little space, a little time was all he'd given up. But the memory of the feel of her thighs around his was motivation enough to arrange their next meeting as soon as possible.

He wouldn't even have to wait for her to confront the Weasel again. Besides, if he interpreted the evening correctly, the Weasel was dead.

Adam had shied away from the logical progression of that thought. Surely Danielle didn't want him dead, too? In any case, he'd refused to consider that negative conclusion and carried on.

Armed with her license plate number, tracing her was child's play, but it was almost divine inspiration that had made him check for a police record. He was fairly sure Danielle would not be pleased to discover he had a copy of it. So how would he find out about the vagrancy charge if he couldn't ask her?

With a grin Adam realized he had yet to discover her occupation. It had seemed like cheating to check the IRS files. The most obvious answer—murderess at large— had been discounted after he'd verified there were no dead bodies lying around the theater. But then, he hadn't really believed she earned her living killing people . . . or had he? Time sped by as he forced himself to return to the bread and butter of his existence, and it was mid-afternoon before Adam had a free moment. He immediately thought of Dani and knew what had to be done.

He wanted to see her, and he wasn't prepared to wait any longer.

SHE HEARD the doorbell, but ignored its summons. Having just put the finishing touches on dinner, she intended to eat it as it was meant to be eaten: hot. Then she planned to enjoy another short nap before it got too late.

She had taken over an hour to fix dinner and was anxiously looking forward to reaping the rewards of her skill and patience when the doorbell rang again. She placed the steaming entrée on a china plate, then flipped off the switch on the wok. It grated on her nerves to hear the bell, and she wished she'd give in one day and have it disconnected. Only members of her family would dream of stopping by without calling first, but they were in Montana. There was no one else she wanted to see.

No one but Adam, and he didn't even have her name. She wondered how he'd get around that obstacle.

On the third ring Dani gave up. The person below was being stubborn, and she had to admit that the light streaming out of the upstairs windows was a definite indication that she was home. It was probably a determined Girl Scout, Dani decided as she skipped down the steps. Just as well, she conceded. She was *addicted* to Girl Scout cookies. She grabbed her purse from the hall table, and one hand was digging for some change as the other turned the knob and threw open the front door.

She should have looked through the peephole, Dani thought, struck speechless to see Adam standing there. She should have known better, should have realized he'd come around at an incredibly inconvenient time. If she'd just taken the time to peek, she could have snuck back up the stairs and kept to her schedule.

Dani could envision a very difficult week ahead. But that didn't prevent the smile that crossed her face before she could stop it. She hadn't doubted he would find her...not really. And even as she admitted she was thrilled to pieces, it was against her basic nature to accept intrusions of any kind. So she dropped the smile and pretended it hadn't happened.

"I guess you're not selling cookies." She dropped the change back into the bottom of her purse, a bit disappointed. It was always fun to see what new variety they were selling each year, although she inevitably invested in the same peanut butter creams.

"You shouldn't open the door without looking," he chastised, pleased that she had. The warm welcoming smile had been brief, but Adam hadn't missed it.

"How'd you know I didn't look?"

"You wouldn't have opened it." Facts were facts, and he knew this was one woman who was more accustomed to discouraging men than inviting their attentions. He'd just have to be more stubborn than Danielle.

He got that much right. "What do you want?" Dani tried to sound unwelcoming, but that was hard to do with the door wide open. She'd have to be more careful about such things. Besides, the part of her mind that worried about such details as schedules and plots was quickly losing the battle to the other part that wondered if he liked stir-fry and Kirin.

She determinedly shut out thoughts of what she looked like in her worn jeans and ratty sweatshirt, not to mention her clean-scrubbed face and ponytail. It was too late to clean herself up. But getting a close look at Adam's tailored slacks and crisp shirt under a casual camel-hair jacket did nothing for her own self-confidence. She looked like she'd just crawled out of the local mission while he looked good enough to eat.

"Invite me in and I'll tell you." Adam was pleased with the progress he was making. She hadn't slammed the door in his face. She wasn't screaming for a cop.

She looked about eighteen in that getup, he decided. But that didn't stop him from liking it. The jeans did great things for her legs, and the sweatshirt was so voluminous it forced him to use his memory. That was okay, though. His favorite recollection was how she had looked in that sexy bathing suit.

"I can't. I'm working. Well, not working," she amended, "but I'm getting ready to work." As if she'd get any work done with her heart going pitter-patter. Pitter-patter! Dani bit back the groan of self-mockery at her teenage reactions to Adam. You'd think she'd never spent any time at all with the opposite sex. Well, she admitted, the last bunch of years hadn't exactly been packed with heavy dates and long weekends in the country. In fact, since college, her male companions had been more on the friendly side than amorous. Anyone not accepting her hands-off ultimatum found himself crossed off her social calendar for good.

Dani had been staring at Adam, her feelings about his arrival a blend of uncertainty and mistrust—highlighted by unmistakable interest. All this showed on her face, but Adam had the remarkable delicacy not to mention it.

"Can I watch you get ready?" What kind of a question was that? he asked himself, hoping Danielle wouldn't notice the unintentionally tacky innuendo. He hadn't meant it . . . not really. Well, maybe just a little of him had meant it. But Danielle wasn't all *that* receptive to him. Not yet, and he didn't want to frighten her off. At least not before she let him past the front door.

Dragging his thoughts back from their detour, he returned to the original premise. He'd asked to watch her get ready. Maybe that would tell him what she did for a living and what that had to do with her rap sheet. Adam was pleased he hadn't pursued the investigation. This was more fun.

Watch her get ready? Dani repeated to herself, then impatiently discarded the vague impression that it had been a risqué suggestion. After all, what did he *think* she did for a living?

"I don't suppose I could convince you to come back next week?" Dani was fighting a hopeless battle, and the only strategy that was worth pursuing was retreat and delay. Perhaps the following week, after she'd killed off all the necessary characters and unraveled the threads of the mystery, she would be able to give him her full attention. He deserved no less.

Adam wasn't disposed to wait. It wasn't a crude reference to his sexual yearnings, although they were ranked right up at the forefront of his thoughts. More, it was critical that he get to know this woman, spend some time with her, find out why she attracted him so completely and discover what made her tick. Whatever he learned would make no difference to the outcome; he just liked to be in possession of all the facts.

It would also be fun to hear about the vagrancy charge.

But nothing that he learned was going to change his mind. He'd figured that out after talking to her in the parking lot. Touching her, feeling the warmth of her thighs as they held his, had only confirmed what his mind told him. He purposely ignored the emotions that accompanied his attraction to her. They clouded his thinking. It was enough to know they belonged together. The details could be sorted out later.

Adam pulled his thoughts back to the present. He couldn't allow her to send him away. He feared that if he let up now, that if he turned his back and walked away at her request, he would be disappointing them both.

4

"I'D RATHER come in now Danielle."

"That's one." *Danielle*. It had been years since anyone had called her anything but Dani.

"I'm sorry? One what?" She'd managed to confuse him. Again.

Dani capitulated. Besides, she argued to herself, she was hungry. "I'll explain after I eat." She turned her back on the doorway, and throwing her purse on the table, led the way upstairs.

Adam tried to make a dignified entrance. Kicking up his heels wouldn't be fitting, but then, she probably wouldn't even notice. Her trim little bottom was already halfway up the stairs.

It occurred to her that she hadn't hesitated to take him upstairs instead of making him stay in the "guest" living room. That only proved how crazy she was, Dani decided, wondering how she'd manage to get anything done tonight. It was vital that she keep up a steady pace in order to finish on schedule, and that would take all the hours of darkness. But it was only mid-afternoon, and maybe she could shorten her after-dinner nap. She was already rearranging her schedule, Dani realized, not at all pleased with herself. But she continued to climb the stairs, only half listening as he shut the front door and sprinted up behind her.

Dani paused momentarily at the door, then pulled it wide open. She didn't have time to reconsider before she felt Adam's hand on her back, pushing her gently into the room and then to one side. He pulled the door closed automatically, then just stood there, his thoughtful gaze taking in every detail of the second floor.

Dani didn't dare to look at the expression on his face. It suddenly mattered very much if he liked her home, and the thought was a novel one.

Taking a deep breath, she rallied and led the way across to the kitchen. "Dinner's getting cold. Are you hungry?" She could stretch to feed two. She always made enough leftovers for a midnight snack.

He stood behind her in the kitchen, the room no longer holding his attention. She'd just invited him to eat. He was in heaven. Adam didn't answer, but looked instead at her feet. She wore socks, no shoes. The top of her head was about two inches under his chin. He grinned, pleased at his previous estimate. Of course, she *was* wearing socks. Barefoot, she might be shorter.

Dani popped a plate full of something into the microwave, then prodded. "Well?" She didn't turn to await his answer, but busied herself with something else that was in a pan on the stove.

Adam looked at his watch. "It's four o'clock," he said, as if time had anything to do with his response.

Dani relented and explained as she tipped the appetizer onto a gold-rimmed plate. Not everyone could reorganize their body clock at will the way she could. "I have to eat now, then I'll nap for a bit. By the time it's dark, I'll be ready to work."

As if that explained anything. If he were a lesser, more suspicious man, he'd be getting some pretty strange ideas by now.

"Terrific." Adam wasn't going to pass up a meal with the woman of his dreams. Not even if she did have a strange schedule. Besides, that shrimp she was fooling with smelled wonderful. "May I help?"

"Get the beer." Dani wasn't sure this was the best impulse she'd had this year. For that matter, it probably rated right down there with the inspiration that had gotten her arrested for vagrancy. But she didn't listen to the warnings sounding in her head. She'd never lied to herself. She wanted Adam. Wanted to get to know him . . . and other things. For the first time since college, she was interested in a man.

But she was still hesitant. Dani knew that part of her hesitancy was prompted by the very real problems of schedule, of time. And furthermore, she was embarrassed. No one had ever managed to witness three murder attempts before. In fact, she wasn't sure she'd ever met a witness of even one.

It might be interesting to get a bystander's viewpoint. Then she remembered she'd also managed to kill Adam. So much for an objective opinion.

Adam reached into the refrigerator and brought out two bottles of Kirin. He didn't bother to hide the widening grin on his face. She wasn't looking. Kirin. How many people in Denver liked Japanese beer? Besides himself, of course.

He followed her to the table, waiting until she had located another place mat before setting down the bottles of beer. As he watched, she neatly arranged the plate of shrimp and a huge bowl of stir-fry something on the table. When she sat down without collecting any glasses for the beer, he breathed a sigh of relief. Danielle was certainly shaping up to be one hell of a woman.

Dani snagged a shrimp from the center plate with her fingers and popped it into her mouth. Garlic shrimp was her absolute favorite food. That and pasta. Any kind of pasta. But this meal had no pasta, so she reached for a second shrimp before the first was past history.

"You said you'd explain over dinner," he prompted, laying the napkin across his lap even as he reached for a shrimp. If this was to be a contest, he intended to win. He *loved* garlic shrimp.

"After," she corrected. Dani grabbed another shrimp, then picked up her chopsticks. She didn't want to talk. She wanted to eat. She was hungry, and at least by concentrating on the food she wouldn't make a fool of herself in front of Adam. She was *very* nervous about doing that. After all, she was out of practice when it came to dinnertime prattle and maneuvering.

Levering a portion of stir-fry into her mouth, she munched contentedly. She'd had a lot of practice at this—eating in silence. Years spent competing with six older—and larger—brothers for a share of the food had ingrained in Dani a silent appreciation of food.

"Oh." A silent eater. That was okay, too. She could explain later. Whatever it was could wait. Adam reached for another shrimp, grabbing two at the same time. He didn't trust her to divide them evenly.

He didn't let himself be distracted by the rice and chicken concoction in front of him. She wouldn't dare take it all, he reasoned. However, the shrimp was another story. Only two pieces remained on the plate.

Their hands collided as they reached for the same piece.

"Wanna fight over it?" Dani challenged.

"How 'bout we agree to a split—one each?" If he didn't put his foot down now, she'd take them both.

Dani pretended to deliberate, then compromised as he'd suggested. But Adam didn't remove his hand from the area until she'd taken her allotment and retreated. He followed suit.

They toasted to the end of the shrimp with the bottles of beer, then turned to the main course. Dani smiled, bowing her head before he could see her expression. This was fun.

And it was a treat not having to explain the rules. She felt they'd been eating together for a lifetime.

She was delighted to see he didn't fumble with the chopsticks; that would have been a major disappointment. There were lots of things she could forgive a person for, but a firm knowledge of the use of chopsticks indicated an appreciation for her favorite food and anything less would have been suspect.

They ate in peace. Dani firmly concentrated on her food, taking pleasure in the familiar textures and contrasting tastes. She loved cooking and spent a great deal of her leisure time in the kitchen. It was always gratifying to eat something she'd prepared with such loving care. And sharing it with Adam made things just about perfect.

Adam agreed. He loved home-cooked food, and eating across the table from Dani was a delightful bonus. He worked his way through the chicken and rice, pausing to delight in the unique flavor of ripe peaches, wondering if that was something she'd made up herself. It made no difference that he'd had lunch just three hours earlier. He finished every bite, then leaned forward to see if she'd left anything in her bowl. No such luck.

"That's one," she started, dabbing the napkin at her lips before taking a healthy swig of the beer. On second thought, she took another sip. It was great beer. "It's an old joke."

"Tell me." It was a joke she took seriously. He gave her his full attention. That is, he listened very carefully as he drank his beer.

Dani leaned forward to rest on her elbows, the bottle of beer within easy reach. She glanced casually around the room as she spoke, only letting her eyes trip over him occasionally. The story would have been seriously garbled if she'd allowed herself to feast on his dreamy blue eyes.

"There was a farmer, his new bride and a mule. They were headed into town with a load of grain to sell. The wagon was heavily loaded, and the mule didn't much like pulling the entire burden by his lonesome. Finally, after pulling the wagon about as far as he could, the mule quit. Just stopped there in the middle of the road and refused to go another step.

"The farmer climbed down off the wagon, walked up to the mule and said 'That's one.' Then he leaned over and whispered into the mule's ear. The farmer returned to the wagon and took up the reins again. The mule pulled the wagon the rest of the way into town.

"After unloading the grain in town, the farmer and his bride picked up their monthly supplies at the general store and loaded them into the wagon. When they were finished, the farmer untied the reins and walked back to climb into the wagon. The mule reached out at the passing farmer and bit his arm.

"The farmer turned to the mule and said, 'That's two.'

"They were about halfway back to the farm when the mule stopped again. He figured the load was just as heavy this way, and those ripe apples in the back looked mighty good to him.

"But the farmer just pulled his shotgun from under the seat and shot the mule dead. 'That's three,' he said as he helped his bride down from the wagon.

"The farmer's bride didn't say anything, that is until he piled a huge sack of flour on her back along with the bag of apples and told her to carry them on to the farm. She refused.

" 'That's one,' said the farmer."

Dani tossed off the last swig of beer from the bottle in front of her and stared at Adam, satisfied that her point had been made.

It was a great story, but Adam was out of beer. He also didn't have a clue what it had to do with anything. He waited.

She told him. "No one, not even my mother, calls me Danielle."

Aha! He saw the light. She hated her name.

"Fine." But he was curious. Danielle was a lovely name. "Why?" He wondered if he tipped the bottle upside down if she'd notice. He tried it.

She took the hint. "Another beer?"

"Yeah." His grin completely covered his face. It wasn't often he relaxed like this, and one more beer would just about shoot him into heaven. Just about.

Dani plucked a bottle out of the refrigerator and brought it to the table already opened. Adam noticed she hadn't brought another for herself, but decided it had something to do with work.

"The name thing?" he prodded, carefully avoiding calling her anything at all as she returned to her chair. Was she going to give him an alternative? He wasn't in the mood to discover if she owned a shotgun.

"My mother used to call me that when I was in trouble. It was the only time she used the name."

"Makes sense." She must have gotten in a lot of trouble to be that adamant about a name. But then, considering what he already knew about her, that was easy to imagine.

"The rest of the time she called me Dani."

Dani. He liked it.

Adam nodded his head in agreement, remembering at the same time the name on her rap sheet was Danielle. No wonder she didn't like to use it. "I'll call you Dani."

"I know."

"Unless you get into trouble," he continued smoothly, knowing full well that Dani's penchant for mischief making was way beyond her own control, much less that of anyone else's.

Dani thought about it, then nodded her head in acceptance of his condition. That was only fair. After all, she had already called him worse—if not actually to his face!

"And you have to call me Adam."

She actually jumped an inch off her chair, wondering how he could possibly know the nicknames she'd heaped on his head since their first meeting. She stalled for a long moment, hoping against hope that when she'd slipped she'd called him Adonis—anything but Pinhead! "Instead of what?" She tried to present the question casually, not daring to look into his eyes.

"Instead of nothing," he returned, slightly puzzled by the question.

Dani's head jerked up, her relieved gaze locking with his amused one. It was that simple, she realized thankfully, he wasn't a mind reader.

"You've never called me by my name," he said softly. "And I think we've reached a point where things like that are important."

Dani didn't debate his words. But it had been so very long since she'd followed this path that she was suddenly shy and speechless. A simple enough request, she knew. But her tongue was having problems getting around the necessary two syllables.

"Say it, Dani," he whispered from across the table. "Say my name."

She was held spellbound by the trance his eyes and voice had woven, and all of a sudden, what had been hard was now easy. She licked her lips, preparing the way, enjoying his attention to her every gesture. It was like performing without acting, she thought irrelevantly. The slightest movement she made gave him pleasure, and it was immediately reflected in his eyes. In return, his every glance, each word…everything he did seemed to be designed to entice her emotions and thoughts.

"Adam." Slightly husky, it finally came out. It was really so easy, she thought, delighted with the obvious pleasure one simple word had given the man seated across the table from her. So she said it again, still softly, unwilling to break the mood at the table. "Adam."

He cleared his throat, a satisfied smile settling on his lips. "That was good, Dani," was all he said. "Very good."

Then Dani prepared herself to ask the question that had been niggling at her ever since she had opened the front door to see him standing there. They'd only met three times before, and the verb "met" was an exaggeration. Dani couldn't decide whether his interest was personal or clinical. For all she knew, he was a doctor specializing in nut cases and demented personalities, but she was confident enough of her own sanity to risk hearing his explanation.

Dani wasn't negating the fact of the strong attraction between them. That would have been silly, particularly in view of their recent exchange. But there was nothing to say his obvious personal interest hadn't been sparked by something more mundane.

"Why are you here?" And once the words were out, she steeled herself against any number of answers. The *last* thing she needed was to hear him say he was a policeman gathering evidence of her criminal activities. But logic pointed out that if he were a policeman, it would be the last thing he'd admit—particularly if he was still in the process of building his case.

Dani didn't really think he was a cop, but worse things had happened to her recently, and the trend was certainly there!

"I'm here because *you're* here," he said simply, "and I want to get to know you under circumstances that are more...."

He faded for a moment, and Dani listened raptly to the silence that surrounded his hesitation, finishing his sentence a dozen ways. More what? More personal? More private? He wanted to get to know her, and Dani was at once relieved and excited. He *wasn't* a cop! More what? More intimate?

"More normal!" he said, a look of pleased accomplishment settling on his features as he found the word he'd been seeking.

"Normal?" Dani was momentarily disappointed. Normal? Just what was wrong with their other meetings?

"Yeah, normal," he repeated, although the last hour had been anything but normal. Quiet, perhaps. Interesting, absolutely. But definitely not normal, at least, not according to any previous definition he'd understood of that word. Adam considered that perhaps Dani's "normal" would be infinitely more exciting than any previous experience he'd ever had with that concept. Words were taking on new meanings around this woman, and Adam wasn't fighting the changes.

He was just fighting to keep up.

"Why do you want normal?" She still wasn't sure she liked that implication. Even Dani realized their previous meetings bordered on the unconventional, but that didn't mean they weren't exciting in their own right.

All of a sudden, Adam realized she had misunderstood. He rushed in to explain. "The other times I was there as a bystander, and I caught you off guard. Yet you *still* responded to me!" He paused, leaning his elbows on the table, a movement that propelled him closer to the bewildered woman on the other side. "The first time, I felt you tremble when I merely touched your wrist." He stopped, marveling over the memory. "You trembled at my touch. I thought about that a lot over the next week, and half convinced myself it was fear because I had caught you doing something you shouldn't have been doing."

Dani was spellbound by the blue eyes that were holding her still and silent. She waited breathlessly for him to continue, knowing that what he was saying was so much more than she had secretly hoped.

"By the time I saw you at the Jacuzzi, I knew better. Your eyes gave you away." He was confident now, not because he thought he'd been wrong, but because she didn't interrupt him to argue. Right or not, it wouldn't surprise him if she argued just for the sake of it. "That's why I followed you to the parking lot."

"Oh." The word left her lips open, the air rushing in and out as she floundered about the vocabulary of her mind in search of something more appropriate to say. But she met with no success and settled with repeating herself. "Oh." After all, saying "How wonderful" or "exactly what I was thinking" was entirely too bold for her. This craving for another's company, for his touch . . . it was all too new, too startling.

"Just 'oh'?" he asked, raising his brows at her brief response. But he was merely prodding her for a reaction, having already learned her real responses from her very expressive face. The attraction was mutual, but Dani was too shy to admit it. That didn't bother Adam. Someday he'd tell her just how exciting that shyness was, particularly in someone who could electrocute two grown men!

Dani wasn't sure what to say next, and elected to return to the practical. It was safer.

"I have to go to sleep now." Dani knew she'd never manage to rest. There was too much unsaid between them. She wanted to know more, needed to know more. Such as, what was it about him that made her heart speed up and sent nervous thrills all the way to her toes?

"You want me to leave?" Adam would do whatever she said. But she had to say it. If the past hour had seemed in the least bit unusual, he put it down to timing. He was intruding upon her life, interrupting a delicate balance. He'd take what he could get.

If nothing else, Dani was honest. Shy, perhaps. Tongue-tied, most of the time . . . at least in Adam's company. But always honest. "No." No, she didn't want him to leave. She wanted to move to the sofa and exchange stories, find out what attracted her to him. Discover why she couldn't get him out of her head. "No, I don't want you to leave," she said. "But I've got a deadline. And a schedule." She avoided looking into his eyes.

It was hard enough saying the words without having to look at what she was throwing away.

Adam gave it some thought. He didn't want to leave, but he respected her work, whatever it was. He'd been in similar corners himself. He compromised. "You go and lie down. I'll clean up here and let myself out." It would be hard to leave. He wanted to stay around more than anything in the world. But it was her home. And her rules.

Dani's head jerked up, and she was treated to the practical, matter-of-fact stare that Adam normally saved for nervous clients. She was tempted. Very tempted. She hated cleaning up the kitchen. And she really didn't want him to leave. Not yet.

"That isn't necessary." She probably couldn't sleep anyway, with him here. "I can do the dishes. I made the mess."

"Please. You cooked. I'll wash up." He reached his hand across the table, covering hers. "You keep to your schedule. I'll stay for a bit, clean up, finish my beer, maybe look around." He took his hand away, not so quickly as to reveal to her the hot sparks that were flaring from the brief touch, yet fast enough to salvage his good intentions. Her fingers were warm, delicate. Adam wished she'd run them through his hair, just once. Maybe not. She needed to sleep.

Dani didn't even worry about having a stranger prowling around while she slept. Adam wasn't a stranger, not really.

Not that she could sleep with her hand on fire. The aftermath of his touch was electric!

"I *like* doing dishes."

She was convinced. After all, how long could it take to clean up? "Okay." She didn't know what else to say. Maybe she'd sleep after he left.

Adam rewarded her with that winning smile for what must have been the right answer, then stood. "What time may I come tomorrow?" He assumed he'd be welcome.

He was right.

"I'll be on about the same schedule all week." Dani didn't hesitate any longer. Adam might have forced his way into her life, but she had no intention of giving him a fight about it any longer. She was delighted he was so determined. And understanding. Besides, as long as she stayed within the bounds of simple attraction, what harm could it do?

"What time will you start to cook?"

"About three."

"I'll be here." That was another hour he could squeeze out of her day without affecting her schedule.

Dani nodded assent, then started across to the bed. She'd only gone halfway before Adam's voice stopped her.

"There are probably a few things we need to talk about." So much was being left unsaid, he realized. Like how there could be such trust between two people who were virtual strangers. And what she did for a living.

"I know." She spoke without turning around. It was spooky having someone read your mind, Dani thought as she continued on her way to the bed. She just hoped he also understood that attraction was the end of the road.

SHE'D SLEPT. The clock was testament to that much. Like a faithful geyser, the alarm sounded at nine sharp, forcefully pulling Dani awake with its clanging bell. She wished she would remember to replace it with something more subtle. She hated the feeling of being jerked into instant consciousness.

She privately admitted that anything less noisy wouldn't succeed in waking her at all.

She was alone in the house. There was an empty feeling that had never been there before, and Dani immediately knew who to blame. Throwing off the sheet, she headed directly into the bathroom for the mandatory shower that would restart the flow of blood and ignite the creative fires.

Just hours ago she'd given Adam rights that had never been granted another man. Leaving him with the dishes, not to mention tacit permission to stay and get familiar with the room at large, she'd pulled the large paneled screen across the platform, an effective wall when one was required. Then she'd disappeared behind it and had done what she'd intended, she'd fallen into an immediate and deep sleep.

She didn't know whether to be surprised or grateful. Or disappointed. She hadn't expected to be able to sleep with someone else in the house, much less a virtual stranger running loose in her kitchen. She'd not heard him load the dishwasher much less let himself out the door.

But she *had* slept, and now she had to work. She owed it to both of them. Stepping out of the shower she pulled on the jeans and sweatshirt she'd brought into the bathroom. Time was wasting, and she had a long night ahead of her.

ADAM SAW the light go on upstairs, followed a while later by several more as she made her way down to the first floor. Good. She hadn't been tempted to lay in bed and give work a miss.

He'd guessed she worked at home, probably on that computer he'd seen in the downstairs office. That would explain the flexibility of her hours, but left a wide range of possibilities as to occupation. He didn't waste any time considering them. Dani would tell him when she was ready.

It had been a snap to clean up the kitchen, although he'd dragged out the process for as long as possible. Then he'd taken the tour, careful to avoid bed and bath area, not wanting to wake up Dani, a bit afraid that she wasn't asleep behind that screen after all. He didn't think he was up to that kind of temptation.

The contrast between the first and second floors gave him something to think about as he sat outside in his car. Adam waited to make sure she managed to wake up.

He never decided what he'd do if her light hadn't come on. Good intentions aside, he wasn't strong enough to waken her to anything less than very gentle loving.

5

IT WORKED!

Dani reread the last paragraph, then flicked off the machine before her enthusiasm could propel her into the next chapter. Time enough for that later. Now, all she wanted was fresh air and sleep.

Changing quickly, Dani let herself out of the house and sprinted down the block. Exhilaration forced her pace and Dani grinned at the pickle in which she'd left Detective McCaffrey. He was the cop who had ended up with the double murder or, as Dani had dubbed it, the Weasel/Pinhead shock. Added to a dozen or so other files on his desk, Dani thought it was brilliant of the man to be able to connect the case to three other unsolved murders, especially with the councilwoman obstructing every step of his investigation. Then the villain was dead, and the mystery was up for grabs.

With a couple of simple changes to what actually happened, Dani had managed to confuse the issue so effectively that the reader was nearly three-quarters of the way through the story without having a clue who had been trying to kill whom. The *why* would come much later. The only problem that faced Dani now was figuring out how to keep Detective McCaffrey alive long enough to accomplish what she needed him to do.

If he survived, Dani was tempted to use him in her next book. She'd rather developed a liking for the lonely, overworked cop.

Of course, there was still the matter of reenacting the villain's murder. With her deadline so near, Dani had opted to go ahead and write in the scene, crossing her fingers that she could accomplish the task in her spare time. As an ironic twist, Dani had decided upon replaying the poisoning scenario. From her own point of view, it would be a snap. Since the villain had been herself, she would have to pick out another victim to kill. All Dani had to do was wander into a bar, pick a victim, doctor another drink, and leave.

Getting away was also important.

And that reminded Dani of Adam. But, then, there was very little that didn't remind her of him. Concentrating on her writing was no small feat, especially with visions of a blue-eyed man distracting her at every opportunity.

Dani admitted her attraction to Adam. Admitted it, but wasn't quite comfortable with it. It had been years since she had let a man occupy her thoughts, years since she had experienced the rush of pleasure at a simple touch. *Attraction.* Dani thought about the word, about how she could control it, limit it. In the cool air of early morning, anything seemed possible. She enjoyed Adam's company, wanted more of it.

In the back of her mind, two more words linked to form a triangle: *attraction, love, trust.* But Dani shied away from the threatening implications. She was strong, she knew better than to give her trust to any man. Never again would she expose herself to the pain and humiliation that trust could provoke.

ADAM FLIPPED THROUGH the typed report for the second time, reviewing the highlights and checking his own conclusions. There was nothing there. At least, nothing he hadn't already known. His top man, Chuck Rogers, sat across the desk from him, drawing silently on the cigarette hanging out one corner of his mouth.

"Do you see anything that I'm missing?" Adam asked him, stealing a look at his watch. Another few minutes and he'd be out of here. His stomach growled in anticipation, and other parts of his body took note of the proximity of the hour. There wasn't an inch of him that wasn't anxious to return to Dani's. Nevertheless, he put his own needs on hold and concentrated on the case at hand. A man's future was at stake, and it was Adam's job to make sure that the man had a future worth living. It was a delicate task, but then, most of the jobs taken on by his private investigation firm were somewhat sensitive.

Chuck shrugged his shoulders, then crushed out his cigarette in the brass ashtray. "It's only been two days, boss," he said, confident that it was just a matter of time before the Channing woman made a move. "We're watching her every second. That is, every second you're not with her," he said with a chuckle, well aware of Adam's distaste for his part in the investigation.

Adam winced, accepting the casual kidding with ill grace. He had objected to the plan from the beginning, but in the end there had been no other choice. Someone had to get close to her, and that someone had to be him. Although the firm was filled with operatives who were ready and willing to take on the job, the case was too important to entrust to anyone besides himself or Chuck, and Chuck's wife had firmly influenced the decision-making process.

"And the post office in Los Angeles?" Adam asked, although he already knew the answer. Surveillance was Chuck's job, and he was as thorough as they came.

However, Adam and Chuck were still mystified as to why their client had been instructed to send the money to Los Angeles, particularly when the suspect lived in Denver.

"It's covered. She can't get at that money without one of our men seeing her. With all those men in L.A., we're stretched kind of tight here, but there aren't any holes." Lighting another cigarette, Chuck slumped back in the chair and stared at the smoke rings he was making. He was good at waiting, much better than most people. "Channing will make a move. She has to."

Adam nodded, then closed the file and threw it down on the desk. There wasn't anything they could do but wait. It was aggravating, especially with the limited time they had left to them.

"Baxter called earlier."

Chuck visibly perked up. Their client was even more anxious than Adam to clear up this mess, and ultimately he was in control of the time factor.

"We've got one more week, then they'll make the announcement." Another week of sticking close to Stephanie Channing. Adam had never imagined time could pass so slowly. Since meeting her at the theater, he'd been with her several times, escorting her to various clubs and restaurants, always in the company of several other people. She liked to be surrounded by a crowd of admirers, and this suited Adam perfectly. He could stay close without having to pretend an intimacy he didn't feel.

Checking his watch for the tenth time, he abruptly stood and began gathering the files and miscellaneous papers scattered on his desk before shoving them into a drawer. "I'll be out for a few hours," he said, reciting Dani's phone number for Chuck's information. It wouldn't do any good for him to be out of touch if their suspect made a move. "Make sure you've got enough men on the post office tonight. I have a feeling she'll be getting desperate for cash, especially at the rate she's been spending. I'm not supposed to see her again until tomorrow, so she's got time to get to Los Angeles and back before then." Locking the drawer with a key from his pocket, he snagged his suitcoat from the closet and walked with Chuck out past the reception desk.

Adam took the long route to Dani's house, driving randomly up and down the peaceful tree-lined streets of Cherry Creek. He was early, but his impatience to see Dani had made it impossible to sit in the office any longer.

It didn't help that there wasn't anything constructive he could do about the Baxter/Channing case. Everything that could be done had been done and now it was a waiting game.

Game. Adam cringed at the word, but couldn't think of a better one. A game of cat and mouse perfectly described their handling of this investigation. The case itself was blackmail. Normally a vicious crime, it was particularly brutal when politics were involved.

A man in California, Jeremy Baxter, was running for political office. Unfortunately fifteen years ago he'd run to Canada after receiving his draft notice.

It was a common enough story, even forgivable if one was inclined to consider the immaturity of the boys who chose this method of evading the draft. Bereft of even political or religious reasons, some just ran because they were horrified at the thought of dying in a dark jungle on the other side of the world.

And now someone was threatening to reveal this lapse in judgment.

It didn't matter that he'd returned to his country under the terms of the general amnesty granted in the seventies. It also wasn't important that he genuinely regretted his actions. All that mattered was that he had acted irresponsibly, and that information could devastate his upcoming election hopes. With the campaign in full swing, he couldn't afford the negative publicity this disclosure would generate.

Jeremy Baxter planned on handling the situation in his own way. Acting upon the advice of his public relations people, he would himself take the responsibility for presenting the facts to his constituency. But timing was critical. While Baxter wanted to get the confession off his chest immediately, his advisors counseled otherwise. If the disclosure was made too soon, his campaign would flounder. But with a secure base of support, they hoped he could use the admission to his own advantage. Baxter was going along with them, mainly because he was pinning his hopes on a future that was designed to aid and serve the country that he'd deserted all those years ago.

On top of this crisis in his career, Baxter was also dealing with a personal conflict. Months earlier, when his father's death had left him a sizable inheritance, he had made a decision to divert the funds to various charitable foundations around the state. Jeremy Baxter was trying, in yet another way, to make up for his youthful blunder. He didn't need the money, didn't want the trappings of wealth and privilege.

He was his own man and was determined to prove it in every way that could possibly matter. Unfortunately his fiancée, Stephanie Channing, had violently disagreed. And when she couldn't sway him from his stance, she'd left him.

Baxter was convinced the blackmailer and Stephanie Channing were one in the same. He just didn't have the proof.

Now, Stephanie Channing was living in Denver, and Adam was trying to find the proof of her involvement in the blackmail scheme. He had been hired by the men who believed in Baxter, a group of experienced politicians who felt the young man could make a difference in the running of the state. They wanted the woman stopped and brought to justice.

Adam had accepted the job because he agreed with them. And now, with just one week to go before Baxter made his revelation, Adam and Chuck were orchestrating a delicate operation that would not only stall Channing until Baxter could make the announcement, but would also provide them with the proof they needed. They had arranged for Baxter to send a token payment, promising the balance when it could be raised. According to the written instructions, it was forwarded to a post office box in Los Angeles.

There was the usual threat that if anyone tried to stop the person collecting the envelope that contained the money, it would bring immediate disclosure of the Canada episode. Adam wasn't worried that his men would be spotted. They were too good at their jobs. But there was a chance that the Channing woman would send someone else in her place, and that called for careful handling of the situation.

The money had been at the post office for two days, and they were still waiting for someone to show an interest. He reviewed the plan, then shut it out of his mind. Nothing more could be done, not without jeopardizing the operation.

With a grin of anticipation, Adam pulled into the driveway of Dani's home, noting with satisfaction that he'd timed it perfectly. She would be expecting him this time, which gave him immense pleasure.

He wanted Dani, needed her in ways he didn't totally understand. It was more than simple yearning for sexual satisfaction, although that was certainly a large part of it. When he thought of Dani, he thought of the future, and that was a concept he needed time to get used to.

In the meantime, some food wouldn't go amiss. Adam shoved open the car door and hurried up the walk.

"PASTA," she said. It was her other favorite. Just in case, she'd make enough so they wouldn't have to fight.

"Great." He wondered if she'd let him have another Kirin.

Adam had arrived promptly at three, this time dressed in the familiar pinstripe. Dani made a note to talk with him about that. It did terrible things for his image. It was a good thing he had dreamy blue eyes or she wouldn't give him the time of day. Then again, perhaps it was a good thing he kept his chest and arms covered with a cloth she found stifling. It might keep her from touching.

Almost as if he read her thoughts, Adam took off the suit jacket, pulled off his tie and rolled up the sleeves of the fine linen shirt he wore. She raced back to the kitchen before he had a chance to see the panic in her eyes.

Dani herself was dressed a little more upscale from the day before. She'd put on a new T-shirt to match a pair of new jeans. She'd even put a bit of makeup on and brushed her hair. That was as formal as she got around the house. Besides, she didn't want Adam to think she'd knocked herself out to impress him...or did she? Whichever, it was too late to change.

Adam appreciated the tight jeans without even giving a thought to her informality. They did wonderful things for her legs, not to mention her nicely rounded tush. And the T-shirt was just as inviting, outlining as it did the fullness of her breasts under the thin cotton knit. Yes, Dani was perfectly dressed for an afternoon at home. He hoped she didn't wear clothes like that outside, then kicked himself for letting jealousy interfere with his appreciation of her perfectly formed body. He'd just have to make sure she wore a coat if she ventured out. A long coat.

"May I help?" It was a toss-up: he could help out in the kitchen, on the off chance he might manage to bump into her a few times, or he could just lean against the counter and enjoy the view. And drink the beer she was bound to offer.

"You eat, you help." Dani took it for granted he was handy in the kitchen. She also needed to get those piercing eyes off her backside and onto something harmless, like a bowl of fresh green beans. She grabbed it in a movement akin to panic, shoving the bowl at him before he could blink. "Clean these."

He was lucky. Cleaning fresh beans was a talent he could boast. He wondered if her expectations would soar if he did a good job.

He was halfway through before he remembered the beer. "Any more Kirin in the fridge?"

Dani wasn't sure Japanese beer was a complement to the meal she was planning, but didn't want to break her concentration by debating the point. "Help yourself." Then, on second thought, "Grab me one. Please." She went back to tossing eggs and flour into the Cuisinart.

She lifted the bottle that he plunked near her work space, and took a long swallow. It was a good idea. Japanese beer was perfect with what they were preparing. She'd put him in charge of beverages from now on.

Dani wondered how many meals she'd get to prepare with his help. There hadn't been a permanent or even semipermanent relationship in her life since college.... She thrust away those memories even as they flitted through her mind. Now wasn't the time to dredge up the past. Determinedly, she pushed the button on the food processor and watched the eggs and flour become dough.

It occurred to Dani that she'd never met a man who had any talent at all in the kitchen, but to be fair, she hadn't known that many men. She snuck a peek over to the sink where Adam was cleaning the beans. Yes, he knew how to clean vegetables, she was thrilled to see.

Not even to herself did she admit that was a rather simple test of skill.

"What next?"

Dani looked up from what she was doing to see him lazing against the counter, beans triumphantly clean on one side, his Kirin held in hand like a trophy.

Dani hoped he could handle turkey. That was the simplest thing left on the list. "There's some turkey fillets over there." She pointed to a cutting board on another counter. "Cut out that white tendon that goes down the middle, then slice each one thinly, about four slices each." She pointed to the knife rack just in case he'd missed the lethal display of sharp instruments, then turned back to her pasta. She'd avoided looking at those eyes. The image in her brain was enough to keep her rattled as it was.

Dani finished with the dough and dismantled the processor after quickly slicing some mushrooms and onions, then stuffed the processor parts in the dishwasher. She covered the dough with plastic wrap to allow it to rest a few moments, then crossed to check on Adam's progress. Approaching his left side, deliberately *opposite* from where he was wielding the knife, she checked out the slices of turkey. It was good news. Not only were they cut to order, but there was no human blood staining the white meat. She was delighted.

"You know how to use a knife." A bit of praise never hurt anyone.

Adam spared her a quick glance, not long enough to be life threatening, then put his eyes back where they belonged—on that deadly sharp knife! He wondered if she spent her evenings running the blades over a stone. He was glad he'd paid the knife due respect from the moment he'd lifted if from the magnetic rack. Was this a hint of some sort? He refrained from trying out the sarcastic reply that was on the tip of his tongue. He pretended she wasn't trying to kill him and chatted casually about dinner.

"What are we making?" He laid the knife carefully on the board, thankful his task was done. Maybe she'd offer to wash it later.

"Fettuccine Alfredo, a variation of Veal Piccata—this time with turkey—and fresh steamed beans for the veggie." She loved this meal.

"Are we going to have to madly cook for the next hour, or can we distract ourselves with talk?" Adam had come to cook *and* talk. He didn't plan on leaving tonight without having learned any more about Dani than he had the previous evening.

She gave it some thought, careful not to look too closely at his eyes. An earlier glance had indicated they were focused on her T-shirt again. She wasn't sure if that was better than having him stare at her bottom while her back was turned. She wasn't even convinced she really minded either.

"We can talk a little now, but not a lot. It distracts me. Maybe after dinner. . . ." She stopped there. He had his own imagination. Let it do some of the work.

Adam shook his head. "No. You said you were sticking to the same schedule. If you have to work, then you need some sleep."

Dani was delighted with herself. Her morning sleep had been more than adequate to last her through the night. She grinned. "I slept extra this morning. I can spare a few hours later this afternoon."

Adam returned her grin. Maybe now he'd have a chance to learn something about her, at least, something more than the fact that she went around Denver pseudo-killing people—a new term he'd made up that seemed to fit the bill—and that she was passionate about food.

It was probably too soon to ask about the vagrancy thing.

Adam reached into the refrigerator, this time pulling out a can of soda he'd spotted earlier, giving the remaining bottles of Kirin a wistful glance. But he shut the door firmly, reminding himself that it was still early afternoon and he'd have to go back to work eventually.

She showed him the flour, salt and pepper, and what to do with them, along with a wicked-looking mallet that was supposed to soften, not kill. He hoped the turkey would be the only victim that night.

"So talk." Dani had no intention of carrying the conversational load. He wanted to talk, he could talk. Maybe she'd learn something.

6

"I'M A PRIVATE INVESTIGATOR," he said, then fell silent before he could tell her more. Dani had to decide for herself whether that was a good or a bad thing to be. He went to work on the turkey.

She wondered if all of his conversations were so abrupt. True, it was an informative statement. It explained why he'd been so quick to interrupt the poisoning attempt at the restaurant; it also explained how he'd managed to learn her name and address. She was curious how much more he knew.

"Then it wasn't a coincidence that you were at the theater?" she asked. "Or the health club?" She turned back to the pasta, releasing it from the plastic wrap and tearing off a small bit. The pasta machine was already in place, and she began to press the dough into long sheets of noodles.

Adam stared at her for a moment, fascinated with her deft movements at the machine. As he watched, she ran the same piece of dough through the press several times, then hung the long strips of pasta to dry on a rack. When she went to repeat the motion, he answered. "It was the only way I could think to find you, by sticking close to the Weasel." Adam didn't tell her the theater *had* been a coincidence, because then she might ask why he was there and that was, strictly speaking, confidential.

"Why didn't we trip over each other before that night at the theater?" she asked, then nearly bit her tongue. The *last* thing she wanted was to remind him to ask what she'd been doing there. But she was curious, because there had been several days between the restaurant fiasco and the aborted try at the theater, and with her literally dogging the Weasel's steps, it should have been impossible to miss Adam.

"I was in New York for a few days, and then it took me a day or so to establish his routine."

"It took me a week to do that!" Dani mentally counted off the days, double-checking the time she'd spent watching her victim. Four days before the restaurant poisoning, another three before the theater. She turned to face Adam, a length of pasta dangling perilously from her fingers. Her nose was slightly out of joint. Had she really wasted all that time?

Adam recognized professional pique when he saw it and suppressed a smile. "But *I* didn't have to try to kill him," he offered. "All I had to do was follow and wait."

Dani was partially mollified. "You're right, of course." She went back to rolling out the sheets of pasta.

"And?" he hinted, holding his breath. He'd been curious about her occupation for most of his life, or so it seemed. He finished pounding the turkey and turned his back on the counter so he could look at her.

"And what?" Dani was fighting with a particularly tricky piece of dough and only gave Adam part of her attention. Or perhaps the dough was being tricky because Adam was staring at her again. She could feel it!

"Why did you have to try to kill him?" He decided putting it bluntly was better than going home ignorant.

"Oh!" She turned to face him again, the pasta forgotten. Dani wasn't impressed with his investigative abilities. He hadn't even discovered what she did for a living. Oh well. Maybe he'd been too busy to do more than get her address. "I write. Mystery novels." There, that explained it. She returned her attention to the pasta.

Adam concentrated on keeping the questions simple. Apparently, her mind made connections that weren't obvious to the synapses in his own brain. She wrote mystery novels and spent her time pseudo-killing the Weasel. He didn't quite grasp the connection between the two.

She'd finished with the long strips of pressed dough, and was altering the handle on the machine to another position. Adam hoped she had time for an exchange of facts.

"What does killing the Weasel have to do with writing?" But as soon as he'd said the words, it began to make sense. Of course. She was like a cook writing a cookbook. All the recipes, or in her case, murders, were tested.

But how did that explain the vagrancy thing?

Dani turned her head in time to see the light dawn in his eyes, then started the next step for the pasta. "You can fill that pot with water for the fettuccine." Did he know about adding oil and salt to the water for perfect pasta? Yup! Dani hid her glee behind an extra turn of the pasta wheel.

Adam read a lot of fiction, particularly spy stories and mystery novels. He'd never read anything by Danielle Courtland. "What name are you writing under?"

Dani was more than a little flattered. He assumed she was publishing, and not just trying to break into the field. "Daniel Carmody."

"Aha!" Her rap sheet flashed before his eyes, and already some of the charges were identified with certain books. Of course he was familiar with her writing. Daniel Carmody was right up there on his list of books—

hardback—to buy the minute they were published. His other list included those he liked well enough, but could stand to wait for the paperbook version.

"Aha?" Dani wasn't following his train of thought.

"Er, yes. Aha!" He frantically sought another response. Mentioning her police record might not set too well at this precise moment. "Aha! *That* mystery writer." He turned to give her that winning grin. "I've got every single book on my shelves at home."

"That only means you have the good taste to buy them," Dani teased. "Have you read them?"

"Every word."

"And?" Dani wasn't above fishing for a compliment.

"You don't need me to tell you they're terrific." His eyes warmed hers with the praise, and Dani was tickled pink. It was fun getting some positive feedback. Hearing the same words from family and agent reeked more of loyalty than appreciation.

"Why don't you set the table," she suggested, the labor-intensive part of dinner at its peak. Conversation would have to go on hold for a few moments. Now that the pasta was ready to boil, she'd cook the turkey and beans, and they'd soon be ready to eat. Dani didn't give him instructions on setting the table. She figured any well-brought-up man would be able to figure out what was needed, and any decent private investigator would be able to find it. She was right.

Adam returned to the kitchen to find Dani caught up in a whirlwind of activity. Standing prudently to one side, he watched as a dozen different ingredients were tossed into one of the four pots on the stove. When she added thick cream and butter to the pasta, Adam winced, silently pledging to add three miles to his run the next day. Oh well. He *loved* high calorie additives.

Moments later, Dani was telling him it was ready. Adam found himself in charge of rotating everything to the table. Each time he returned to the counter, Dani would shove another bit of something into his hands for transport. It was only after he'd transported a dish of Parmesan cheese and a bottle of wine—Chardonnay, she'd chosen—did she follow him to the table.

"Pour and eat." En route to the table, she had slipped off the scarf that was holding her hair out of her way and brushed the flour from her arm. Barely controlling her delight at sharing yet another meal with Adam, Dani slipped into her seat and flicked her napkin onto her lap. She was well aware that a bright flush of excitement stained her cheeks, and she hoped he would chalk it up to working over a hot stove.

He took the wine, filled the delicate goblets he'd placed hopefully on the table just moments before, and followed her example. Although there looked to be plenty, he knew better than to trust her good nature. He spooned his share onto his plate and began to eat.

About ten minutes later, as he took time out to refill their wine, he gave her the compliment she deserved. "It's terrific." Enough said. Back to eating.

Dani nodded between bites. She'd waited all day for this.

The serving bowls were bare and both dinner plates were clean before they took a break.

"Do you always eat like that?" She couldn't, he knew. Not and keep a figure like hers. He studied what he could of that figure from where he sat. It wasn't easy. Her hair covered most of her back and then fell in ripples from her shoulders to rest on her breasts. The golden waves were caught in the beam of sunshine emanating from the sun bubble above the kitchen and glistened magnificently.

Adam ignored the sudden thrumming in his veins and concentrated on the conversation.

Dani didn't say anything for a moment. Instead, she made patterns in the Parmesan cheese left on her plate, not daring to look up and catch those blue eyes staring at her. It was hard to lie when one was being studied so thoroughly.

Dani didn't figure she knew Adam well enough to admit to the six-week-long fast-food binges to which she occasionally succumbed. That was one of her best kept secrets. Not even her parents were aware of her addiction to mass-produced onion rings and pancake-thin hamburgers. She threw everyone off the scent with the gourmet cooking and fitness routines that were more the norm than not.

"I exercise every day. So I can eat like I want once a day." Dani wasn't really lying; just stretching the facts.

"What do you eat the rest of the day?" Adam was interested in this diet. Eat what you want, especially food such as they'd just partaken, and lose it all with a bit of exercise. He was lucky if he could eat like that twice a week and hold the line. She crossed her arms, obscuring his view of the results of her fabulous diet.

"Nothing."

"What do you mean, 'nothing'?" Everyone had breakfast, then lunch, not to mention occasional snacks, he thought. Dinner was just another part of the routine.

"Nothing. Well, almost nothing. I drink that instant protein stuff for breakfast along with gallons of coffee, no sugar or milk. Lunch is rarely more than fruit or celery or something munchy. All energy." She finally raised her eyes to see if he was taking her word for it. In this case, she was telling the truth. Dinner *was* the only real meal she ever ate. Whether it was stir-fried chicken or tacos from the nearest drive-thru, she only ate dinner. True, with the hours she sometimes kept, she could schedule dinner for any hour of the night or day. She quite often ate dinner at eight o'clock in the morning. Dani was grateful for the extended business hours of fast-food establishments.

His expression told her he believed her. Almost. His eyes also indicated they were thinking about something quite different.

"There's got to be something else to this diet," he insisted. Lots of people skipped breakfast, munched healthy stuff at lunch and didn't snack. Very few of them looked like Dani.

She smiled. "I don't often tell people the rest of the secret. It makes the diet sound too hard."

Adam leaned his elbows on the table, prepared to hear the very worst. After all, if she could do it, so could he. It was the only chance he'd be able to eat this way every night. It never occurred to him that he wouldn't get the opportunity. Dani wasn't exactly showing him the door. There was hope. "Tell me."

"No dessert."

His face fell. This wasn't going to be as easy as it looked. "No dessert?" he asked, half afraid his ears had heard her say "no dessert." Impossible.

"No dessert. No sweets of any kind. No chocolates, no peppermints, no cake or ice cream. Nothing." She smiled compassionately, knowing he'd been confronted with a rather large stumbling block to joining her rather eccentric diet. "Except the chocolate stuff I drink at breakfast," she amended. "I can't stand to drink it unflavored."

"Not even whipped cream on a coffee drink?" Adam was stunned. She was changing his whole way of life.

"Nope." She didn't bother to tell him she didn't particularly care for most sweets anyhow. That would make it seem as if she was cheating. Doughnuts didn't count...they were mostly dough. And Girl Scout cookies...they were only once a year.

He leaned back in the chair, sipping the last of the wine from his glass as he thought about it. Outside of the no dessert rule, it was a very acceptable diet. Eat little during the day. Well, that was no problem for his schedule. He often ate only because it was the hour for it. And the rewards were infinitely greater than the sacrifices. He could have dinner with Dani at night. At least, he hoped he could. It was time to find out.

"All right," he said, nodding his agreement. "I can manage that."

Dani jerked her eyes up from their contemplation of the highly polished silver knife that lay on the table beside her plate, a deep red blush coloring her cheeks as she met his stare. What did he expect her to say to that?

"Dishes?" she was adept at changing the subject. However, his knowing grin didn't entirely miss her feeble attempt at stalling.

"Dishes." Adam pushed back his chair and was around the table, pulling Dani's back before she realized he had moved.

"Thank you," she said, hugging the glass-topped table with all the desperation of one who needed an anchor in a storm. She avoided his touch in this manner, then reached to help clear the dishes. She shivered in disappointment at the missed contact, then had to tighten her grip on the fine china as he reached from behind to grab a bowl and platter. His fingers brushed her bare arm, just lightly, then went on to their appointed task.

She nearly died from the sparks his touch generated. So much for mild attraction, she mused. She was electrified.

Adam moved deliberately, setting the china serving pieces on the counter before returning to the table and picking up more dirty dishes. He carefully avoided touching her again. His knuckles were singed from their last brush with her silken skin. Perhaps if they weren't juggling expensive china he'd have taken his chances on another accidental contact. Maybe after dishes.

On his return trip to the kitchen, Adam skirted the space where Dani was working. If he was any judge, she had jumped just as high as he had at the light touch. He looked forward to sharing coffee with her.

The phone rang, and Dani shifted some of the dishes closer to the sink. It rang again as she reached to turn on the tap.

"Want me to get that?" Adam wondered if she liked to let her phone ring a dozen times, just to make the caller aware they were interrupting.

"No, thanks." Dani smiled kindly at his offer, then started to fill the sink with sudsy water. The phone continued to ring.

"Aren't you going to answer it?"

"No."

"I left this number with my office." He hated to admit it, especially since she appeared determined to ignore its summons.

"Oh. Then go ahead and answer it," she encouraged him, thrusting her hands into the hot water.

Adam turned back to the living room, his eyes raking every tabletop and cushion. It wasn't immediately obvious.

"In the bedroom," Dani said from behind his back. She was carrying a towel, trying to avoid dripping suds onto the polished wood floor. "That way." She motioned carelessly toward the screens. Adam tore off across the floor, counting the eighth ring just as he picked up the receiver.

Dani went back to the sink, shaking her head. If it was her parents on the phone, she'd let Adam make the explanations. They were the only ones who called at any given hour of the day or night. All her friends were aware she was busy working this month, and would rather die than bother her. And her agent wouldn't call at all. She was a survivalist.

"It was for me."

"That was lucky," she said, flashing a relieved smile. "I don't have time to entertain my parents."

"Parents?" Adam didn't understand what that had to do with the phone call. But then, nothing with Dani was immediately obvious. She made you work for the answers.

"Yes. They're the only ones who'd call me right now." She explained how she could eliminate her friends and agent from possible callers.

"Why would you have to entertain them? Where are they?" It wasn't getting any clearer.

"They live in Montana," she said, reaching for the frying pan she'd used for the turkey, eyeing it with distaste. She hated doing the pots and pans. Adam decided to divide his attention between talking and drying the dishes, then rummaged through three drawers before remembering the clean towels were over by the sink. Sensible place for them to be, he admitted, wondering why the simple things escaped him in Dani's presence.

"Let me see. Your parents are visiting here from Montana, and you're avoiding them by not answering the phone." Adam was proud of his logic. It made sense, although he didn't think the answer quite fit Dani's way of doing things. He really didn't think she'd choose such a subtle way of ignoring someone. More likely, she'd just come right out and tell them they were interrupting.

"No, silly," Dani laughed as she handed him the clean pan. "They're still in Montana." She wondered how Adam got such ludicrous ideas. Imagine! She'd never ignore her parents, or anyone else from the family. She loved them too much.

Adam took a deep breath, dried the two dinner plates, then tried again. "Then why would you have to entertain them if they're still in Montana."

"Because if a man answered the phone, they'd be here before dark." So there, smart guy.

Finally! The bell rang in his head, and Adam wondered if he'd get better at these games with practice. "Are you saying they're overprotective?" He didn't mind that. Family was important.

Dani moved over to the stove to scrub and polish. It had been a messy meal preparation, and she had to work at it a bit. But she took the time to answer. "No. Not overprotective. Just caring." She didn't know how much to tell him, because even a little would expose the pattern of her life. She decided it didn't matter. He'd find out anyway.

"A man has never answered my phone." She turned to face him, dishcloth forgotten on the counter. Her eyes sought his as she told him what he wanted to know. "I've never taken a man home to my family. And, outside of a few close friends who don't figure into the category we're discussing, no man has ever been in this room."

Adam kept his distance. No man, no lover had been in this room. It followed that no man had been in that huge bed behind the screen. An image flitted across his mind of the two of them, legs and arms twined as they lay exhausted on that incredible bed in the aftermath of a sensual adventure. He'd sat on that same bed while talking on the phone with Chuck. It gave him pleasure to know he'd be the only man to share it with her.

The honesty of her words was a far cry from the usual male-female games he'd played over the years. He wondered if she knew just how important her answers were to him. Suddenly it occurred to him that she might be warning him off. He had to know. Now, before it was too late. Then he realized what a useless thought that was. It was already too late.

"Dani, I'm here because, among other things, I want to be your lover. Not just your friend." She'd been honest. It was his turn. But he held back the whole truth from her. This wasn't the time...she wasn't ready to hear what he wanted to say. "If that idea doesn't appeal, tell me to go. Now." His chest tightened in agonizing dread. All the excuses about sexual attraction he'd made to himself over the past few days were meaningless now. True, he wanted Dani. He wanted her in his arms. But more important, he wanted her in his life.

His instincts had been telling him this for days. After their confrontation in the parking lot, Adam had half-heartedly tried to convince himself that it was merely chemistry between them. But he could no more ignore the truth than he could deny his love for her. Now his heart and soul were finally listening. Adam wasn't altogether sure he'd ever be able to leave—even if she told him to go.

When would he ever get around to telling her he loved her if she asked him to leave now?

Dani nibbled on her lower lip, stalling in the face of his blunt demand. This was harder than she'd anticipated. She hadn't expected him to put it into words. They were startling. And exciting. They made her shy and tongue-tied. But she'd started this conversation, and it was important to them both that she finish it.

"No," she whispered. "Don't go."

It was settled.

Adam consciously loosened his fingers from the pan he was drying and set it beside him on the counter. Three long steps brought him to where Dani stood. He noticed she had to tilt her head back to keep her eyes locked on his. It exposed the smooth length of her neck . . . and her pulse beating erratically at her throat.

"I've never even kissed you," he murmured huskily. "How do you know you want to go to bed with me?" He had her backed against the counter, trapped without lifting a finger.

"I didn't mean . . ." She started to protest, breaking off into silence as she saw the reprimand in his eyes.

He shook his head slightly, one end of his mouth curving up into a smile of reproof. "Don't lie to me, honey."

Dani licked her lips slowly, moistening them to compensate for the sudden breath that left her open mouth in astonishment. He was so sure of what he wanted, what *she* wanted, she realized. It was hard to believe another person could read her mind so thoroughly. Of course she wanted to go to bed with him. But that was just the beginning.

She wanted to make love with him, not just share sex. Love. Dani repeated it to herself, absurdly calm with her admission. When had *that* happened? No matter. Logically, Dani knew it couldn't be real. It was only part of the formula, and the missing link—trust—was something she still controlled. Without that all-important item, love was merely an extension of the attraction she felt.

She lowered her chin as she took another breath, only to have it raised again with the slight pressure of his finger.

"Don't be shy, Dani," he coached softly, misinterpreting her hesitation. "It's too late." The motion of her delicate pink tongue had brought him one step closer to losing his control, but he held himself tightly. There were other things he wanted to know. They were important, perhaps not for tonight, but certainly for their future nights together.

"Is there someone else?" he asked with an outward facade of calm curiosity...and if this wasn't nearly the most important question he'd ever asked someone. Not that it mattered, he granted silently. But he wasn't in the mood for complications. Not now. Not now that he'd found the woman who made his universe complete.

Dani started with surprise. "No. Of course not." Men like Adam weren't exactly falling at her feet these days, she mused. Even so, she doubted if she would notice them. None of them were Adam.

Of course not. Simple for her to say, he thought. Nothing like an easy answer to put him off his stride. So he threw out his next question without preamble.

"Are you a virgin?"

He expected a blush and he got one.

"No."

His finger kept her chin from lowering again. "Don't hide from me," he commanded. "I'm not trying to embarrass you. I just need to know. For your own sake."

She believed him. And her statement about not having men in this room *had* been a bit misleading. It's just that it had been such a long time ago, way before she moved to Denver. Dani recovered from her shyness and held her head more firmly, looking him straight in the eye. "It was a long time ago. In college." That's all he needed to know.

"Thank you." He didn't want, nor did he receive, a detailed history of her sex life. That wasn't what he was after. But what she just told him revealed a lot. He hadn't dreamed that Dani could be a virgin, not in this day and age. But her open, unpracticed response to him had aroused his curiosity. Not untouched, but relatively inexperienced. Adam found he liked the combination.

"It's not just sex. With you, I mean." Dani felt she had to tell him that what she was feeling was more than lust, more than the need to satisfy her most basic desires. But she couldn't bring herself to use the word *love*. He would misunderstand, read more into it than she meant. Then she would have to be honest and explain the bit about trust, and that would probably confuse him. For that matter, Dani wasn't at all convinced *she* understood!

"I know." Adam had his confidence back now. Of course it wasn't just sex. But he'd tell her about the wedding later. Maybe in a few days, after she'd gotten used to having him around. After they'd talked enough to figure out why it was love that drew them together, not just sexual attraction. He hoped they wouldn't have to talk *too* much. Dani's conversations were normally a bit hard to follow, and he didn't want to concentrate too hard. Not now.

He palmed her face in his hands, his thumbs tracing the line of her cheekbones. "Open your mouth." He lowered his head, then stopped, his face just millimeters away. "Please. I want to taste you."

Dani gasped, involuntarily following his instructions. His tongue thrust deeply between her teeth, finding her tongue, drawing it out. It didn't occur to her to resist. This was what she wanted, what she'd been waiting for. His mouth moved skillfully on hers, showing her the way when she would falter. His tongue searched out the moist cavern, tickling the roof of her mouth, polishing the rows of teeth before withdrawing to allow his lips to move gently, then firmly on hers.

With his free hand he caressed the side of her face, touching the fine planes, the delicately molded cheekbones, the intricate curves of her ear. A slight pressure at the side of her jaw, and her mouth opened readily under his. He again pushed his tongue past her teeth and tasted deeply. The kiss was no longer questioning; it was demanding. Their tongues met and dueled, caressed and toyed.

Her hands fell without conscious thought to his shoulders, steadying herself, giving her fingers a touchstone with reality. Because the pulsing ache between her legs wasn't real, just as his matching hardness was an erotic fantasy. Then Adam began a fierce thrusting pattern with his tongue that drew their bodies closer, her breasts crushed his chest, arms wrapped tightly as if their very closeness could relieve the throbbing deep inside.

Dani's breathing was erratic; she inhaled when she could, existing on the air that he gave her, returning the favor so he wouldn't have to break away. His teeth nibbled on her lower lip, his thumb massaging the tiny hurt as he moved on. Then his hands moved to pull her even closer, and Dani stretched her neck farther so as not to lose contact. Adam compensated for the difference in their heights by pulling her to the side so that she lay on his arm, her hair draped in a gleaming curtain, leaving her body open to his gaze.

He did more than look. He touched. With his mouth sealed again upon Dani's lips, his fingers sought and found an already hard nipple beneath her T-shirt. Nothing less would do. With only his mouth, he'd aroused her to a panting, wanting state. He needed to touch what he'd caused to harden. His fingers tightened on the tip of her breast, careful not to brush against the rounded swell that was straining against the knit of her shirt. He wanted to put his mouth there first. He disciplined himself, giving her the maximum pleasure using a minimum of touching, because if he touched too much, he wouldn't be able to stop. And he had to stop. Soon. Chuck needed him at the office within the hour.

Adam lifted his mouth from hers, noting that her open eyes were glazed with passion, her lips swollen from his kisses. It pleased him to see the tension she'd displayed the other night was gone, replaced by an unreserved response to his touch. How he wanted to satisfy those yearnings! But time was limited, and he wanted their first joining to be perfect. They'd have to wait until later, when work didn't cause them to part unsatisfied.

Her breathing was out of control. Dani wanted his lips to come back and make the hurt go away. Because she did hurt. Dani hurt with all the passion that had lain unawakened for years. And now he'd managed to let it loose with one kiss. Well, one rather excellent kiss, she had to admit. His fingers tightened on her nipple, just to make sure he had her attention, then moved to the next. Dani held her breath, waiting. She felt so good she hurt all over.

Adam, too, waited as his fingers teased and tortured the hardened buds. It wasn't enough. She lay easily against his arm as he leaned against the counter for support, her hands clasped around his neck, her head thrown back.

"I need more." His voice was nearly unrecognizable in its husky demand. He checked her eyes for a protest, not that he expected one, then firmly grasped the fabric of her T-shirt and pulled it to rest above the full globes of her breasts.

Dani froze in his arms. From decently covered to half-nude in less time than it took to think about it. And Adam wasn't thinking; he was looking. She watched his expression as his eyes devoured every square inch of exposed flesh. Then his fingers released their grasp of her shirt and drew a firm line between her breasts, not stopping until they reached the snap on her jeans.

"I want to see you naked," he breathed. "All of you." But his hand stopped, and he straightened, just slightly. Dani didn't hear the moan of frustration that left her lips. Adam did.

He took a deep breath, then another, coaxing his body into a more relaxed state. But it was a difficult task, particularly with Dani still in his arms. Letting his hand rest warmly on the smooth skin of her belly, he answered the questions in her eyes. "Not today. We can't."

It was next to impossible to feel composed in her position. So Dani settled for shattered. It had been so many years since she'd allowed any man to come so close, close enough to touch, to taste. And she had her own needs, her own desires. She needed to run her fingers through the light mat of hair she could just see under the fine cloth of his shirt. She needed to rub her breasts against him, to feel the beat of his heart against her own.

She needed to feel him inside her. This most of all. And then, perhaps then she'd be able to understand just how she'd come this close to a man she barely knew. And barring understanding, she'd maybe just be able to accept.

But with his denial, she felt neither of these. Not understanding, and certainly not acceptance. She made a movement to pull down her shirt, but Adam was faster. He held her hand away, his eyes asking for something she didn't understand.

"I have to go back to work," he said. "I'm sorry."

The sigh of relief came out undisguised. Work. She could relate to that. But first, she had to deal with a measure of anger. He didn't release her from his hold, from his scrutiny, and Dani was simply too small to fight back. So she attacked verbally from a position reeking with vulnerability.

"So why did you spend all this time winding me up?" Dani was pleased with herself. She almost sounded objectively curious instead of boiling mad. She wasn't used to the sensual extremes Adam was introducing. They frightened her.

"I needed to touch you." It was the truth.

"So you touched. Now let me go."

"I'm not finished." Adam didn't like the look in her eyes, the one that signaled anger. But that didn't stop him from wanting to enjoy just a little bit more of her delightful body. He'd deal with the anger later.

She thought he was going to kiss her again, and clamped her mouth tightly closed in firm rejection. He licked his lips, his tongue slowly drawing across their fullness, his eyes daring hers to follow. He didn't kiss her.

Instead, his lips sought a hardened nipple. Her back arched in uncompromising response to the feel of his mouth on her tender flesh. His lips moved, skating wetly over the fullness of her aching breast, his tongue laving the creamy skin as it followed the natural contour. Then he moved to the other, giving it the same attention as the first.

Dani was lost in a wonderfully erotic world of Adam's design. She shivered uncontrollably when his teeth nipped delicately at the tips of her breasts, then shuddered as his tongue glossed over the tiny sting. And when he released her hand so that he could palm the curve of her breast, her fingers wound themselves tightly in his hair, pulling him closer.

With a regretful sigh, Adam placed a final kiss on each of the glistening peaks, then lifted his head, his eyes finding Dani's wide with unsuppressed desire. And then, a flicker of remaining anger.

"I won't apologize." He raised Dani from her semireclining position, holding her at his side as he looked over the top of her head at the clock on the stove. Then he turned and put both hands at her waist, lifting her easily to sit on the counter before she'd regained her footing. She tugged the shirt over her breasts, and Adam was more than a little relieved. It wouldn't do to take another taste. He wanted to exite her with words now, not actions. Honesty worked with Dani, Adam knew, and he calculated his next words carefully. They were intended to diffuse the anger. It would also be nice if he could leave her with a few erotic thoughts about the following afternoon.

"If I didn't care about you, I'd be deep inside you at this very moment. Here, in the kitchen. If I wanted, I could have taken you standing up against this counter. You wouldn't have stopped me. Even though we'd never made love before, I wouldn't have hesitated to take what I need." He paused to watch the blush that was becoming so familiar as it darkened her complexion. "Because that's what I want now. To be inside you, to feel your softness surrounding me."

She looked away, no longer able to watch the hunger in his eyes without responding to it. Dani shuddered at the image he presented. He was right. It was only because of his own control that they weren't satisfying the desires of their bodies.

"But I'm not going to sacrifice what we have in favor of satisfying my own lust for you. Even if I took you now, I'd still have to be out the door in five minutes. That's not right."

"Then why did you...?" She trailed off, unable to say the words. Why did he tease her so, touch her in a way that made her ignite like a brushfire out of control?

"I couldn't leave without touching you. I had to taste your skin, feel your softness against my lips." He was standing between her parted legs, a position that was reminiscent of the night in the parking lot. He had a fantasy about that particular position, but today wasn't the time to tell her about it. That could wait. Adam touched the side of her face gently, coaxing her to meet his eyes. "I couldn't go another day without knowing how you'd respond to my touch."

"And?" Dani understood his curiosity immediately. She had the same questions about him. Unfortunately she was no closer to the answers.

Adam smiled, enjoying a subtle satisfaction at her interest. It was a promising beginning. "Your response to even the most innocent caress is utterly astounding. And

when I touched your nipples with my tongue, you nearly
shot out of my arms."

His fingers traced a circular pattern on the inside of her
elbow as he spoke, and Dani had to concentrate on
breathing in the face of such erotic stimulation. His
words, his touch left her totally without a will of her
own.

"Considering the relative restraint of my caresses so
far, I honestly think you'll be mindless when I get serious about making love to you," he whispered into her
ear, not able to resist the obvious signs of her renewed
arousal. He went on to give her a brief description of just
a couple of things he planned to do to her, delighting in
the shudders that raced through her body. He didn't
bother to mention his own response. That was totally
obvious, and not a little uncomfortable. Nevertheless,
his tongue reached out to trace the shell of her ear, then
his teeth nipped at the lobe before he remembered. Time.

"I've got to leave." He removed his hands and stepped
back.

Dani looked at him a bit wildly, then made a con-
certed effort to regain her control. But she didn't jump
down from the counter. That would put her too close,
and her rattled senses dictated a measure of caution at the
moment. He was leaving. She couldn't even speak.

"I'll be here at three tomorrow," he said, not giving her
a choice. "Don't plan to cook. I'll bring something."
Adam wasn't about to spend another two hours cooking and eating. She'd just have to make do with whatever he could pick up between here and the office.

She nodded. It sounded like a good plan to her.

He didn't say goodbye. He didn't even trust himself to
kiss her one last time, not with those passion-filled eyes

hugging his every move. He just grabbed his tie and jacket, slinging them over his shoulder, and left.

Dani listened to his steps as he made his way to the ground floor and let himself out the door. Then there was silence.

She wondered how on earth she was going to write with every nerve ending still sizzling from his touch.

But Dani skipped her nap and went straight to work. Her heightened sensitivity added a new dimension to the novel. She hoped her editor wouldn't mind.

7

ADAM DIDN'T SHOW UP the next day. Not at three o'clock. Not even at four. Dani refused to allow herself the luxury of worrying. She had a schedule to keep. He'd either forgotten their date or was tied up by business.

She didn't know him well enough to decide which. And she convinced herself that she didn't care.

At least she pretended she didn't. When her dinner hour had passed without any food being consumed—Adam had promised take-out—she pulled a can of soup out of the cupboard and heated that. Along with some French bread she kept in the freezer, it made a credible meal.

She threw most of it into the garbage disposal.

Dani had worked all night, then well into the morning. After a much-needed run, she'd found time for just a couple of hours sleep before Adam was scheduled to arrive.

But he didn't come.

Too tense to nap, she wandered around the house, suddenly dissatisfied with the privacy and silence that had once brought her so much comfort. Now she felt adrift, her body rhythms disrupted by outside forces she couldn't control. She should have been feeling satisfied. The writing had been going very well, and she was within a day or two of finishing.

So where is he? she asked the silent room, then stopped herself. He was a grown man and could take care of himself. He hadn't asked her to worry about him, and she didn't have time for it anyway.

Dani opened the door that led to the ground floor and trotted down the stairs. Her office welcomed her return to the gloom and quiet, and in no time at all the computer was humming. If she couldn't settle down to sleep, she could write.

It had always worked before.

IT WAS TEN O'CLOCK the next morning before Dani shut off the computer with a satisfied groan of weariness. It was done. Well, mostly done. She still had to do basic format and printing along with some minor editing, but that was a snap and could be done anytime.

She'd also take time to reread the last few chapters. Two hours of sleep out of the last forty-odd didn't guarantee a perfect manuscript. But she knew it was basically sound, and that was all that mattered.

She had spent the entire evening, all night and most of the morning writing because she didn't know what else to do. Worry wouldn't get her anywhere, and anger clogged the creative cycle. So she'd zeroed in on the book, typing the occasional garbled sentence every time her undisciplined heart clutched at a sudden thought of Adam.

Stretching, Dani fell back into the soft cushions of her chair, a sudden inertia claiming her body. Now that the writing was done, there was nothing to keep her worries at bay.

Memories from another time in her life had been bothering her all through the night, and Dani was irritated at the parallels that seemed to jump out at her. But avoidance was only making her feel worse, so she pulled out the facts and did her own comparison.

It had been a long time ago, in her last year of college. She had been working toward her degree in international relations when she and Greg had formed their close friendship. Greg was also studying for the same degree, and the relationship blossomed rapidly, nurtured by endless hours spent together, studying, researching and, finally, loving. It was Dani's first sexual experience, and if she didn't find it to be as "consuming" as was described in romantic novels, she hid her disappointment well.

It was during the last semester that things seemed to go wrong. While Greg made vague noises about absenting himself in order to pursue his own research, Dani spent countless hours reading and researching for her term project. She finished typing the final copy a week before the due date, then went in search of Greg. She'd been so involved in her work that his recent lengthy absences had not bothered her. But now she was ready to take up the threads of their relationship.

She found him in the arms of the campus beauty. It hadn't been difficult, even with well-meaning friends pointing her in the opposite direction. Dani easily read between the lines and looked into the shadows of their misguided pity. She avoided a public confrontation, but the private one was nearly as mortifying. Behind the closed doors of her room, Greg's pitiless listing of Dani's shortcomings—an unflattering description of her less-than-enthusiastic response to his sexual advances—had been a humiliating lesson. He coldly told her she was hopelessly frigid and her lack of warmth had driven him into the arms of a woman who appreciated him. Dani's own inexperience in these matters prompted her to accept his accusations as fact. It was a truth that formed the basis for the solitary pattern of her life.

She discovered his second treachery the following day. Not only had he rejected her for another, prettier girl, he had also taken her research project. And he'd managed to pass it off as his own. The professor, unable to withhold his praise of the work, had complimented Greg in front of the entire class.

Dani learned the hard way that trust, lightly given, was never valued. She also learned two other very important things. She learned that she could write, quite well in fact, and write fast, even when personal aggravations were making her tense and insecure.

She also learned that she preferred her independence, and had no intention of giving that up again for any man. Never again would she let someone close enough to take advantage of her. Never again would she give a man her trust.

On the practical side, she spent five days revising the basic premise of her research, now presenting an opposing argument to her original thesis. It was simply a matter of employing debating tactics—taking the side you were assigned and presenting it to the best of your ability. Dani succeeded admirably, grimly aware that it was her talent for writing and quick thinking that had saved her standing in that class. It was a lesson she wasn't soon to forget.

Her first book was mailed to the publisher six months after graduation. She hadn't looked back since.

And in all those years, any inclination to trust the opposite sex was suppressed by the scars from that first, disastrous experience.

Adam was the first man to slip by her self-imposed barrier, and he'd managed that with little effort. Dani knew she'd made it easy, her immediate attraction to him making his advances nearly effortless. The humiliation she had suffered from Greg's accusations was obscured by one very basic fact. She responded to Adam. That is, she responded *sexually* . . . without reservation. Logic pointed her to the only possible conclusion: she had been cold and unresponsive with Greg because there had been no real attraction between them. It was a completely different matter with Adam.

Dani decided against analyzing the emotional response that went along with the sexual one. It was like arguing about which came first, the chicken or the egg. And without trust, she wasn't even sure it was important.

Dani didn't have much dating experience, so when Adam didn't appear as promised, it was too easy for her to remember Greg's infidelity. But even as she compared the two, she knew better. Where Greg had been a boy, Adam was a man, with a man's responsibilities. And she tried to convince herself that she wasn't nearly as vulnerable now, not like the girl she had been at twenty-one. That she wasn't hurt, just angry.

He can make you angry, she told herself, *but he can't hurt you. No one can hurt you if you don't let them.*

Dani forced herself up out of the chair, wobbling slightly on unsteady legs. What she needed now was sleep, lots of it. Instead, she climbed the stairs to the second floor and dug out the yellow pages. Flipping to the section on Investigations, Private, she slowly read through the listings, not relying too heavily on her ability to spot his company on a random chance. Her eyes were too tired to gamble, so she let an unpolished fingernail guide her way. She hoped the listing carried his surname. Without that vital clue, she didn't have a chance of tracing him.

She needed to find out if he was hurt, or whatever. She couldn't sleep until she knew. If he was okay, she'd go to bed. Of course, after she got some rest she could always kill him herself. It would serve him right for worrying her to death.

It was there, in the second column. "Winters and Associates. Private Investigations." Dani tore out the page and took it over to the phone. She couldn't have carried the whole book, so she saved her energy for the important stuff. She concentrated on dialing.

"Winters and Associates. Good morning." A pleasantly calm voice answered on the second ring. Dani nearly hung up the phone. If he was dead, the voice at the other end wouldn't possibly sound so composed, so reassuringly cheerful.

"I'd like to speak with Adam Winters, please." Dani was polite. It wasn't the voice's fault if Adam was a no-show.

"I'm sorry. Mr. Winters is in conference at the moment." The voice paused, then asked, "Is there someone else who might be able to help you?"

"Is he alive?" That's all Dani needed to know.

"Yes!" came the startled reply. The voice lost a great deal of its practiced calm. "Of course he's alive."

"Thank you." Dani replaced the receiver, then unplugged the extension.

She knew what she needed to know. The rest—whether he'd stood her up or had been detained by business—well, that was a matter of lesser interest.

He was okay. She could sleep.

ADAM CLOSED THE DOOR behind him, then stood quietly, allowing his eyes to become accustomed to the dimness. She'd lowered all the curtains, and efficient blocking screens had been pulled across all the sky-lights. He moved to her bedroom, taking care not to make any sound. He didn't want to frighten her.

She was there, just as he'd known she would be. Asleep, of course. That explained the telephone problem.

Adam breathed a sigh of relief, the devastating sense of loss he'd experienced the last few minutes fading, leaving him limp and exhausted. He stood at the foot of the bed, drinking in the sight of her still form, wondering what giant leap of logic had made him panic in the first place. He'd been afraid she'd gone, left her home so as to avoid him when he finally returned. But the egotism that supported that theory slapped him in the face, making him realize that his place in her life wasn't yet important enough to cause her to completely change her schedule and routine just to evade him. He reassured himself with the important part of that sentence: not yet! With the loosening of tense muscles, Adam took a moment to admire the abandon with which she slept.

She was lying sideways across the bed, not lengthways as one would normally expect. The exceptional size of the mattress allowed her to stretch out completely, and this she did. On her back with her arms over her head, reaching in abandon away from the rest of her body, she unconsciously opened herself to his thirsty gaze. Masses of blond hair concealed most of her face, and he let his eyes wander down to feast on what was revealed to him. Seeing her clad only in a skimpy silk thing, he was at the same time enticed and frustrated. The nearly transparent material hid nothing from him. Not the darkened tips of her breasts, not the shadow at the juncture of her thighs. Her legs, long and perfectly formed, were caught clumsily in the sheet.

He caught himself tensing up again and stopped. Dani wouldn't appreciate the abrupt awakening his body was demanding.

Adam distracted himself by looking out the window. It was midday out there, yet no light intruded into the room. Studying the glass more closely, he saw all the windows in the room were made of material similar to that used in cars to screen out the sun's rays and to prevent curious eyes from seeing more than vague shadows. Ingenious.

He stood there for several minutes, alternately surveying the room and allowing his eyes to rest on the soundly sleeping woman. He was going to stay with her of course. Leaving her alone now was not even a consideration.

He hoped Dani didn't stay angry too long.

When Annette, the receptionist who had taken Dani's call, mentioned the strange conversation she'd had earlier with an unknown woman, Adam knew immediately who had called. He'd dialed her number, only to listen to an interminable number of rings before he gave up that tactic. Either she was determined not to answer, or she was gone.

But she was just sleeping. He moved closer to the bed, then noticed the cord on the table beside the telephone. She'd disconnected this extension. Of course. She hadn't wanted to hear his excuses.

Adam admitted Dani had a right to be angry. He was nearly a day late in showing up for their date. But that was something they'd deal with later. Dani wasn't the only one missing out on sleep. Quietly, so as not to disturb her, Adam pulled off his sweater and shirt, tossing them carelessly on one of the chairs beside the bed. Then, he sat on the bed to remove his shoes and socks, careful not to crush the foot that stuck out of the sheet on that side.

Turning slightly, he studied the problem of where to lay his own tired body. Eliminating the less attractive proposition of trying out the sofa, he rose and crossed to the other side of the bed where there was about three feet of available space. Just as he was going to lie down, Dani flipped over onto her tummy and slid laterally about three feet, managing in that simple movement to appropriate the small section of mattress that had previously been vacant. Adam suddenly understood the rationale behind the size of the bed, grateful this was one thing he wouldn't have to ask her. He could just imagine what she'd do with that question!

Adam studied the new arrangement carefully, taking great appreciation in the sight of Dani's bottom, only partly covered by the silken teddy. Wondering if the sofa in the front room weren't possibly a safer choice, he went around to the other side of the bed and quickly claimed a piece of the mattress for himself. He shut his eyes with a relieved sigh, not bothering with the sheet that was wound around her legs. He didn't need it. His thoughts were keeping him nicely warm as it was.

Adam was tired, exhausted by worry and worn down from the lack of sleep. Lying beside Dani was not only a temptation, it was a relief. He concentrated on the latter, not fighting the waves of sleep that rose to claim him.

DANI KNEW she wasn't alone the instant she awoke. It wasn't a difficult assumption to make; her cheek rested against a very warm body, one that was breathing quite regularly.

It didn't occur to her to feel threatened. Waking up with one's head pillowed on a man's chest might be a bit startling, particularly if you were used to sleeping alone. But Dani knew this man, and she controlled her reactions admirably.

Without moving her head, she opened her eyes to verify her thoughts. Right on the first guess, she saw, recognizing Adam's chin from a familiar angle—above her! But not for Dani was the terribly romantic luck to wake up cradled in a man's arms, her cheek nestled on his broad chest. No, she was a bit off the mark for that. For one thing, Adam's arms appeared to be flung out above his head. For the other, her head was resting quite comfortably on his stomach.

As if to confirm her present location, a distinctly unhappy rumbling sounded directly under her ear.

"I'm famished."

Dani jerked upright, stifling the scream that threatened. He was awake. She scrambled to the other end of the bed and cowered there on her knees, one hand reaching up to drag the uncombed mass of hair out of her eyes. It was enough to remain calm while she thought he was asleep, but awake he presented a very definite threat.

"You're late." It occurred to her that she was supposed to be angry. Dani had never been stood up before. She didn't know how mad she was supposed to get, or for how long.

He was here now. He'd come back. She tried not to let her delight show, realizing that any outwardly welcoming gesture would weaken her side in whatever argument they were supposed to conduct now. Dani was at the same time thrilled with his presence and irritated with her own lack of faith. Shoving aside all thoughts of Greg and those lonely years since college, Dani concentrated on the situation at hand.

Adam pulled himself up to rest against the headboard, working on a casual approach to her statement. The sight of her kneeling there, just a few feet away, was distracting. Very distracting. Her breasts pressed against the fragile lace, their tips beckoning him, reminding Adam of their delicately firm texture. And with her knees spread on the mattress for balance, she was an exciting picture of feminine enticement. He'd soon let her know just how much he appreciated the view. But first, there were a few problems to get out of the way.

"I'm sorry. You're right, I'm a bit late. It was unavoidable." Adam reflected on her use of the word *late*. She didn't accuse him of standing her up—a logical conclusion under the circumstances. Evidently Dani didn't measure time like normal people. That was okay with him, particularly as it might help him out of this spot. She was either *very* understanding, or *very* angry... and hiding it reasonably well. Adam decided he didn't want to find out which. Not yet. So he changed the subject.

"Dani, next time you call the office, give Annette your name."

Annette, the voice. "Does the poor dear have trouble remembering the girl of the week?" Now why had she said that? Dani fumed, not liking the catty flavor of her words. But she was still suffering from the long hours of worry, and it was hard not to lash out. Anger, she reminded herself. It was only anger. He didn't have the power to hurt her.

Adam refused to rise to the bait. But he was curious about the wounded expression that crossed her face. "No, honey. It's just that she would have put you straight through to me."

"Why? Have I made it to a list of preferred callers?" Dani realized she had progressed beyond the point of sounding catty, but she couldn't seem to hold her tongue. The idea of sharing Adam with other women angered her very much indeed. "I won't be one of many."

"Don't be silly," Adam said, his voice a bit more gruff than necessary. Didn't she know what was going on between them? He'd make sure she had more confidence before he left her alone again. "I wouldn't have gone to all the trouble of breaking in here if you hadn't given me reason to worry about you."

That brought up another point. She guessed it was her own creative imagination that had relegated this matter to the ranks of minor annoyances. Breaking in was something she wished she knew how to do. "I shouldn't let you get away with that. Breaking and entering isn't exactly the proper way to come calling." Dani purposely didn't come down on him too hard, hoping she could someday convince him to show her how he'd done it. Had he used a credit card to get past the lock, or did he have more sophisticated tools?

Adam felt the adrenaline slip into his bloodstream, a vivid reminder of how worried he'd been that morning. "If you'd answered your phone, it wouldn't have been necessary," he said more loudly than necessary, then grasped a fistful of the sheet and threw the end in her direction. "Cover yourself. I can't talk sense with you dressed like that." He couldn't even *think* with her dressed like that.

Almost reluctantly, Dani reached out for the covering and pulled it up to her neck. She liked having his eyes on her. It made her feel wanted, a nice change from the rejection she'd been imagining. But Adam looked more interested in yelling at her than anything else.

Perhaps it was because she didn't have much experience with men, but she just couldn't bring herself to hold up her side of an argument, and his scowling countenance clearly indicated that was where they were headed. And for the life of her, Dani couldn't see that *he* had a thing to be annoyed about.

"Answer me one thing." Dani tried to bring an end to the fracas before it started. "Why didn't you come earlier—like you promised?" If he had forgotten, she'd learn it now. If there was another woman, he'd tell her. Dani's stomach tightened as she waited for his reply.

"It was work. I couldn't come. I couldn't call." There had been a burst of activity at the post office in Los Angeles, and Chuck and Adam had flown there to direct the investigation and surveillance of the new suspect, a man using the name Sam Holbrook. A discreet search of his apartment had revealed a definite link with Stephanie Channing, but their elation had soon diminished when Holbrook made no move to deliver the money to the woman. Once again, they were forced to wait.

He couldn't explain any of this to Dani. Not now. There was such a thing as professional confidentiality. He knew she had been worried. Her comments to the receptionist about his health had not gone unnoticed. Perhaps someday she'd learn to trust that he could take care of himself. And even if this particular case wasn't on the risky side, there would be times his safety depended upon his total concentration. He couldn't afford to worry about Dani, not and survive. But if his occupation was going to come between them, he needed to know. It was what he did for a living, what he enjoyed, what he was good at.

Dani tried desperately not to show her relief at his answer. If there had been another woman, if he'd simply forgotten, he would have told her. Pressures of work she could easily believe. "Will that happen often?"

"No," he said. "Not often."

He hadn't said never. Dani understood what he meant, but that wasn't to say she liked it. The fear and the uncertainty of the last couple of nights were certainly not something she wanted to experience often. But it would take time to convince Adam that giving her a few details would save them both a lot of anguish.

Dani nodded, at once accepting his explanation and plotting her own campaign.

Adam had been studying her hands as they clutched the sheet to her breasts. His eyes lifted to meet the determined acceptance in her gaze. Good. They had an understanding. But Adam still had a few points to make.

"It's important that you don't unplug your phone, and that you answer it when it rings."

"Why?"

"Because I worry about you when I can't get through. That's what happened today. You didn't answer, and I imagined something was wrong. That's why I broke in."

"Why should you worry about me?" Dani liked the feeling. Adam was here, in her bed, because he'd been worried. But wasn't that carrying things a bit far?

"Because I can't help it." *Because I love you.* But he only said the first part out loud. Adam didn't think she was ready for the rest of it. She smiled at his admission, though, and it was enough. He repeated his request. "You will answer the phone when it rings, right?"

"If it's that important to you. Yes, I will." She refrained from asking him to call so she wouldn't worry. They'd just been through that. It seemed to Dani that the worry load was a bit lopsided.

He didn't look angry anymore. In fact, Dani was beginning to think he had something quite different on his mind. Shyness overcame her as she watched his gaze turn hot and smoldering. It dawned on her that they'd talk better over coffee. In the living room. Dressed. Dani suggested as much. "Coffee? Food?"

"No." It just occurred to Adam that he'd spent nearly six hours in the same bed with Dani, sleeping.

"Then why don't you sleep while I eat?" she suggested, knowing that *she* was the sleepy one while *he* was the hungry one. So much for logic.

"I don't think so, Dani." The soft growl warned her, but she skirted the issue, shy at the implication, unbearably tempted by her own wants and needs.

"I need sleep. I've hardly had any in two days." Dani stalled. She'd just been having a practical conversation with this man. It wasn't that easy for her to change directions that fast.

"We can do that later. You're okay for a couple of hours."

A couple of hours? She panicked. "I'm hungry. *You're* hungry." Dani was scrambling for an excuse, any excuse. She wasn't ready for this, not for what she read in Adam's eyes.

Adam was aware they still had a lot of talking to get through. But there was time for that. The important stuff had been gotten out of the way. Deliberately he reached for the crumpled sheet and began to pull. Slowly. "Now, love, either come here, or let me look at you," he commanded huskily. In truth, he wanted both. He wanted her to come to him, and he wanted to look at her.

It was the same sheet he'd tossed at her earlier. Dani had a choice. She could maintain her grasp of the sheet, and let herself be dragged ignominiously across the width of the mattress, or she could let it go, allowing him a view of her hardened nipples beneath the teddy.

He tugged, she held on. His eyes searched her face for a clue as to what she was thinking, and stumbled on the surprising answer. She wasn't playing hard to get. It wasn't the coy game of a woman practiced in the art of seduction. Dani was shy, he realized, stunned with the discovery. He remembered the woman who had shuddered in his arms just the other day, and how she'd held his mouth to her naked breasts. Oh, yes, there was passion there, Adam knew. Passion stifled by an incredible, adorable shyness.

He dropped his corner of the sheet and jackknifed off the bed. He'd go to her. Another time she'd have the confidence to come to him willingly. For now, he'd show her how easy it was to do.

Dani was momentarily stunned when he left the bed. For a split second, she feared he was leaving the apartment, leaving her. Then he was behind her, warm hands resting lightly on her bare shoulders, brushing aside the heavy locks of hair that tumbled in disarray. She tried to turn, to look at him, but he held her firmly in place.

"Relax, honey," he said, knowing full well it wouldn't do any good to tell her that. Adam braced his legs firmly against the corner of the mattress, his toes digging into the plush carpet, and pulled her to rest solidly against him. Still on her knees, her head came halfway up his chest and, with his hands resting on her shoulders, he pressed her closer. Warmth was important for security, and he gave her his.

A full-length mirror that stood near the bathroom passage reflected their images, the evening shadows lending a dreamlike frame to their figures. He saw that Dani had shut her eyes. He was fairly sure she hadn't noticed the mirror. He smiled, enjoying the sight of his hands as they lightly caressed her fragile neck and shoulders. He'd make sure she opened them later.

Adam continued his gentle massage, silently debating how to approach her. He wanted her fully aroused, totally excited *now*. To match his own need. His fingers slipped under the straps of her teddy and pulled them off her shoulders, tugging at the fabric until it was at her waist, trapping her arms against her body. Her breasts were bare to his hands, and he immediately sought their fullness.

She tried to turn again, but he held her firmly between his hands and his hard, lean body. It was frustrating. It was exciting. He'd taken the first step, and now Dani wanted to take the next. "Let me touch you," she whispered, then gasped as he took her nipples between thumbs and forefingers, gently plucking at them. She fell limply against the support his body offered. Nothing, absolutely nothing had ever felt this good.

Adam continued to tease the buds of her breasts, thoroughly enjoying the sight of what he was doing to the woman he loved. In the mirror, he watched Dani arch under his ministrations, her slender arms still caught in the lace teddy. Then it wasn't enough for Dani to passively accept his caress. She pushed aside the silken bonds and reached back with both hands to grasp the strong muscles of his legs, frustrated to find the barrier of his trousers instead of the heated skin she sought. The movement thrust out her breasts, and Adam was compelled to take a deep, stabilizing breath. She was so beautiful he wanted to bury himself deep inside her without waiting another second. But he was determined to wait. He didn't want Dani aroused. He wanted her mad with wanting.

"Dani," his husky voice penetrated the sensual fog that surrounded her. "Dani. Open your eyes." Her hands rose upward to grasp his forearms, perhaps for balance, perhaps in a desire to direct his touch. And as she opened her eyes and focused on their mirrored images, Adam saw her expression change from startled surprise to an uninhibited enjoyment of the picture they presented.

"Oh!" It was all she could say. The sight of Adam's hands on her breasts with his fingers gently massaging her hardened nipples excited her more that she would have thought possible. But what he did next sent her even further into the seductive fantasy that Adam was creating. A single hand left the breast it had been fondling, gliding slowly across the velvet firmness of her belly. It came to the lacy material bunched at her waist where his fingers drew long, sensuous lines across the top of the silky barrier.

Then Dani watched his hand disappear without warning beneath the silken covering, and arched back as his fingers immediately began to comb through the nest of curls that guarded her most secret place. Her lids started to close as she gave herself fully into the sensations he was arousing.

"Keep your eyes open, Dani," he breathed into her ear. His practiced fingers pinched a nipple a bit roughly, demanding she pay him attention. "I want to see through your eyes what you're feeling. I want to know your excitement as I get closer to your warmth."

So she opened her eyes, though the effort was nearly more than she could afford. She first looked at the reflection of his face and warmed herself in his gaze of smoldering desire. Then his eyes lowered to the silk curtain, and she followed.

Skilled fingers moved upon her then, discovering for themselves the damp warmth of her body, and Dani heard herself cry out in wonder. A hot wave of burning pleasure slammed through her, then again and again. She whimpered at the force, defenseless against each erotic invasion.

Adam's eyes took possession of hers, memorizing the results of each stroke of his fingers, of the subtle pressure of his thumb. And when he knew that she was beyond any vestige of control, when her body alternately slumped and arched against the support of his, only then did he give in to his own desires.

With a swiftness that divulged the immediacy of his needs, he pulled Dani away from the security of his body and turned her around, lowering her down to the mattress. The silk teddy disappeared down her legs just as his trousers were shucked and discarded.

Then he was inside her, driving deeply, without restraint. He drew her legs up high around his waist, and plunged harder, deeper. And Dani responded completely, wildly. She arched to meet his every thrust, holding him to her, dragging her nails across his back in an exquisite torment to his control.

Adam held her firmly to the bed, mastering her wildness, reveling in the complete lack of inhibitions with which she responded to his every move. Her soft cries penetrated the quiet of the room, turning to pleas when he would hold himself back. He leaned forward to taste her breast, sucking the nipple into his open mouth, creating a maze of sensation that electrified the woman below him. He partially withdrew from her, a tactic necessary to guard his own self-control, and she begged for his return.

"Now, Adam," she begged. "Please." She couldn't take any more. Adam agreed. Lowering himself to her again, he took her mouth with his tongue, invading it with the same rhythm that he thrust his manhood into her hot, silky core. Then she was exploding into a million bits, falling back to earth just in time to catch Adam as he shouted his own joyous completion.

Two bodies, slickened with sweat, clung together on the massive bed in the last shadows of dusk. It was done.

The last morsel of self-doubt was erased in the aftermath of their explosive lovemaking. Breathless whispered words of amazement and satisfaction were shared. Sentences were half formed, only to be interrupted by a lazy kiss, the play of tongues, an exchange of air.

Adam nuzzled the damp hollow behind her ear, reveling in the memory of their perfect union. Dani's response, both emotional and physical, had topped his wildest dreams. It was no longer feasible to contemplate a future without her.

He examined the situation methodically. On his side, he knew he loved her, enjoyed her company, approved of most of her tastes and preferences and was physically drawn to her—if one could use such mild terms to describe his passion for her! Her rather unique approach to her work, her diet, even her rap sheet—all these he could accept, for they were what made her Dani. He was even convinced he could learn to follow her conversational patterns. And even if he couldn't, he'd learn to dodge the more obvious pitfalls!

He could only surmise how Dani felt about him. He thought she liked him, was assured she was physically attracted, and she did seem to enjoy his company. Going back over the bare facts, he frowned slightly, realizing there was something obvious missing. Dani wasn't yet in love with him. But he pushed such doubts aside. Given the chance, he was positive she'd fall in love—especially if he provided the appropriate atmosphere.

Maybe she'd marry him first and let him work on the rest after the formalities? After all, his love for her was enough to build on!

Adam decided to give her a week. Then he'd ask her to marry him—whether she was ready or not. Satisfied with his decision, he tightened his arms around the subject of his thoughts and brought his attention back to the present.

"Sleep or food, love?" The husky whisper was ignored by Dani as she lay beneath him, the exhaustion that claimed her body making it impossible to reply.

"Sleep, then," Adam decided agreeably. Anything that would allow him to keep Dani in his arms was okay with him. Carefully drawing away from her, he pulled himself to the center of the bed and propped a couple of pillows behind his shoulders. Then he reached for her and pulled her to rest on top of him. She was so light he scarcely noticed the weight.

"You can't sleep like this," she protested hazily, her head comfortably cradled on his chest. Her legs fell to each side of Adam's, his still-hard masculinity lay cradled against her belly. This was nice, Dani thought, beginning to doze off.

"You're right," Adam agreed. "I can't sleep like this." Then his hands were at her hips, and before Dani was aware of his intentions, he was inside her again, as hard as before, equally as welcome.

She tightened around him, arching against the wildfire excitement that rushed out of nowhere, some of the sleep starting to leave her.

"No, Dani," he chuckled. "Not yet. Just sleep for now." *Well, perhaps just a short nap,* he amended.

No? Dani looked at the closed eyes, then settled herself more comfortably. If he could sleep, well, so could she.

Maybe.

8

"I DON'T SEE why we couldn't just send out for something." Dani was loathe to make a mess in the kitchen. She was also starved for a heavy dose of MSG, and that meant take-out. Unfortunately she couldn't use that particular argument.

"Because they only deliver fast food around here," Adam reasoned, wishing at the same time they could just order a pizza loaded to the gills. But he knew better than to suggest such blasphemy in this house. Maybe he could marry Dani and still keep his fast-food fetish a dark secret.

Dani pulled a sweatshirt down over her head, taking note that Adam was lying there on the bed, just watching, leaving his own dressing for another time. It unnerved her to have the man pay her such close attention, and she quickly pulled down the soft material to cover her breasts. It was a big sweatshirt, and Dani felt safe from his prying eyes inside its loose folds. And with the hemline halfway down her thighs, it adequately camouflaged the fact that her jeans were next to indecent. But they were her last clean pair, and Dani decided they were better than no clothes at all.

"Well, if you don't want a cardboard pizza or frozen Chinese, you'll have to move it." Dani flipped her hips at his inert form on the bed, and made for the kitchen. "You either help in the making or clean up later all by your lonesome."

Dani didn't have the faintest idea what to cook. It was hard to get excited about filets or escallops when your stomach was craving onion rings and pizza. If Adam stayed around much longer, she was simply going to have to come clean about her fast-food fetish. She tried to picture a scenario that would ease him gently toward the idea of an occasional hamburger or pizza. She was still standing in the kitchen, staring at the various appliances, when the phone rang.

Adam, instantly triggered into work mode, flung himself over to the other side of the bed to catch it before it rang again.

"Did Dani say you could answer the phone?" were the first words to come across the line.

It was interesting for Adam to discover from whom Dani had inherited her conversational abilities. "No, ma'am. I just answered it." Adam knew who he was probably talking to. One, it was a long-distance call. Two, Dani had already warned him friends and agent were guaranteed to leave her alone this week.

Not that this sounded like any mother he'd ever met. The soft husky voice was a mature variation on Dani's own sensuous speech. Adam firmly believed in the adage that a man should look to his wife's mother to discover what she'd be like in the future years. She passed the voice test.

"She didn't say I couldn't, though," he offered.

"Is she there?" As if, perhaps, Dani was not in her own apartment with a male that took liberties with the telephone. Maybe she thought he was the plumber.

"Yes, ma'am, she's in the kitchen. Er, would you like to talk with her?" Stalling for time, Adam tried to come up with a clear and concise way to present his situation. Nothing came immediately to mind.

"Eventually, if it's no trouble." Dani's mother sounded amused at his speech problems.

Although he wasn't prepared for it, Adam was glad to have this opportunity to talk with Dani's mother. It might be the only chance he got before the wedding.

"My name is Adam. Adam Winters," he said, diving right in before he could lose his nerve. "Dani and I are, er, seeing each other," he finished lamely. He ignored the peals of laughter emanating from the kitchen. If Dani objected to his talking with her mother, she could very easily come into the bedroom and take over the phone. Until then, Adam was taking advantage of having a future mother-in-law on the line, particularly before she'd had a chance to form any concrete opinions about her future, and unknown, son-in-law.

"Beatrice Courtland here, Adam."

He liked that. Instant first-name basis, from a woman he suspected never used first names unless her arm was being twisted. Perhaps it was.

"Pleased to meet you, ma'am." He couldn't bring himself to call her Beatrice, not yet.

"Dani is our only daughter, Adam." Beatrice wasn't exactly beating around the bush, he noted. "We do, however, trust her judgment." Going less on what she said than how she'd said it, Adam knew she'd made the jump in logic that Adam was most likely enjoying some sort of intimate relationship with her daughter. She was correct.

Adam turned his back to the kitchen, effectively blocking his conversation from Dani. She didn't have to know everything. Not yet. "I'm very much in love with your daughter, Mrs. Courtland," he said. "I plan to tell her about it when she's ready. And before she has a chance to get used to that, I'll be married to her."

And without a pause from the end of the line, "How soon do you feel she'll be ready?"

Adam relaxed. Mrs. Courtland, Beatrice, either approved or was humoring him. Whichever, the cooperation suited his purposes. "Maybe next weekend. At worst, no later than the one following."

"You'll let us know?"

"Of course."

"We'd like to be there, if possible."

"If possible, I'd be delighted to have you." But if he had to drag Dani to the altar, he'd just have to save the introductions for another time.

"Has Dani mentioned she has six brothers?"

Adam gulped in recognition of her rather less-than-subtle warning. Beatrice Courtland was a formidable opponent—particularly when backed by bone-breaking ammunition. There was a significant lull in the conversation before she asked to speak with her daughter.

Adam motioned for Dani to come to the phone. Threats he could deal with, but convincing Dani they were on the road to something worthwhile suddenly took on a more urgent timetable.

He sincerely hoped Dani wouldn't hear of their marriage plans before he'd had a chance to put them to her himself.

Dani waltzed across the room, slipping the receiver from his slightly weak grasp and mouthed "Had enough?" before directing her more vocal comments into the instrument.

"Yes, Mother." Her tone was indulgent, obviously loving. Adam admired her poise, knowing how close she was to her family. It couldn't be easy to talk with your mother when she'd just had a conversation with your lover.

"No, he's not."

Not what? Adam wondered. Certainly Dani wouldn't lie about their relationship. Beatrice Courtland didn't sound like the type of woman one lied to and got away with it.

A pause, then, "Perhaps."

A longer pause, a chuckle. "I'll let you know." Dani turned to grin at him, then said, "Yes, Mother. You'll be the first." A few sounds of caring and love, and she put down the receiver.

"You'll be the first what?" Adam asked before Dani's hand had left the receiver.

"The first to know if I'm coming home for Thanksgiving," she said, a tiny grin tugging at the corner of her mouth. She had deliberately phrased her responses to her mother's questions, knowing Adam was listening to every word. Served him right for turning his back so she couldn't eavesdrop from the kitchen.

Adam tried not to look relieved. "She didn't ask you about me being here?"

Dani laughed. "I don't know where you grew up, but my mother would rather die than embarrass me with a question about my living arrangements."

Adam pondered that, added it to what he already knew about Dani, then stated flatly, "You've never lived with anyone before."

"True." Dani thought about his statement, then added. "But we're not exactly living together."

"Would you like to?" he asked casually, as if this were merely a conversation and not an incredibly important step in the right direction. Living with Dani wasn't precisely the end goal he had in mind, but it was a start. Particularly as her mother had already given tacit approval . . . that is, pending his proposal of marriage during the next few days. Adam rose from the bed, the sheet that had been covering his lower torso falling back to reveal his interest in their conversation. The idea that they might soon be living together was an incredibly arousing one, Adam realized as he moved in Dani's direction.

"No!"

Dani drew away from the vicinity of the bed, nervously backing out of the room. It was a reflex question, she knew, but it had caught her off guard. Adam was teasing her, responding to her own mood. But somehow Dani wasn't laughing.

Commitment and trust. Trust and commitment. The words were almost interchangeable, and the arrangement suggested by Adam required a lot of both. Or was she thinking of something else? Logically Dani could accept that living together didn't represent a commitment. In fact, all it really implied was thrift. One house, one apartment, not two.

Either way she wasn't interested. She couldn't afford to be.

"I haven't lived with . . . a man . . . before." Dani stuttered over the words, then found herself cornered in the bathroom, the only escape blocked by the man she sought to evade. It seemed easier to explain why she hadn't, rather than why she wouldn't.

"I know you haven't," he said, deliberately tracking Dani into the sumptuous room with the giant shower. "Not yet. But I asked if you would like to. With me." Although her initial reaction had been negative, Adam pushed the subject a little further. Not because he thought she would change her mind, but because he wanted her to know he was serious.

Dani stood mute, tongue-tied at her inability to repeat her original reply. She wished he would quit teasing her before she made a complete fool out of herself and said yes.

"That's a big tub," he nodded toward the blue monstrosity in the background, changing the subject when she didn't answer. He let his mind roam, creating endless fantasies about the two of them covered in a mass of bubbles. Dani stood there, visibly confused, on the verge of starting an argument. Adam knew it would only take a touch there, the pressure of his lips elsewhere, and she'd say yes. He could kiss her confusion away.

But he didn't. Dani deserved better from him. "Which do you recommend?" he asked, indicating both the bath and the shower with the sweep of his hand.

Considering the obvious state of his arousal, his invitation was unmistakable. If Adam had thought to dispel her confusion, he wasn't doing a very good job. She was speechless. Did he seriously think she'd strip down and jump in the bath—or shower—with him? Dani then shocked herself by giving it consideration. But the next moment she looked up to find his eyes resting gently upon her tingling body, the laughter not so well hidden that she couldn't see it. A deep red flush climbed up to completely cover her face, a proper accompaniment to her mortification.

"Alone, Dani," he leaned forward to run his knuckles across her heated cheeks. "I wasn't suggesting anything. I'll just get clean real fast and come help with dinner. We both need to eat." And maybe an ice-cold shower would relieve his frustration, Adam hoped. Burying himself deep inside of Dani would have been a preferable option, but he didn't want her to think he would use sex to pressure her into changing her mind. And coming right on top of their discussion about living together, she might very easily believe he was trying to force a decision.

Still, there was a note of hope in his voice when he suggested, "Maybe another time?"

"I hope you drown," she said in as steady a voice as she could manage, then slipped away without touching him. Dani didn't know which was worse—listening to his muffled laughter or admitting she'd have given anything to "get clean" with him.

Maybe later, when she took her own shower. She was cheered by the idea and completely forgot her anger. Teasing was good for a relationship, she decided.

Revenge also had its place. Dani went to work in the kitchen.

IT WAS LATE, but neither Dani nor Adam paid any attention to the hour. The irregular demands they'd made upon their body clocks the last few days had completely thrown off any hope of regaining their normal sleep cycles in the near future. So they just went with it, relaxing in the soft light of a single lamp, lounging companionably on one of the overstuffed sofas.

The entree of spaghetti bolognaise had been accompanied by French bread, liberally spiced with garlic and loaded with butter. For a meal that came entirely out of the freezer, it was the best spaghetti Adam had ever eaten.

"It's the freezer," she explained when he asked about her secret recipe. Naturally, as far as Dani was concerned, that explained everything.

It didn't.

Adam sighed and wondered how much he wanted to know the answer, the full answer. But he was intrigued by the bait—that's what he was calling Dani's unintelligible answers to any of his questions. Bait. And it worked every time.

He took it. "What's the freezer?"

They were sitting, well, slouching, together with Adam's arm resting on Dani's shoulder. She had to twist her head to get a good look at his face, and gave him the opportunity to see the mischief in her eyes. "It's that big appliance next to the refrigerator, silly."

He sighed heavily, dropping his chin to his chest. This wasn't going to be easy, especially if she insisted upon making it a contest. Then he let the chuckle rise and escape, admitting, silently of course, that it would be interesting to see how long it took before he started winning. Not all the time, but just enough to salvage his ego. "That was awful."

"You asked for it." Dani snuggled closer, taking care not to spill any of the Chianti from her glass.

There was a long period of silence before Adam reluctantly pursued his original question. He still didn't have his answer. "So what does the freezer have to do with your spaghetti recipe?"

"Everything. Spaghetti sauce tastes better after it's been frozen. In fact, *all* Italian food tastes better that way."

"I suppose you've got a dish of lasagne just waiting to be cooked or reheated or whatever." Adam was planning tomorrow's menu.

"Yup."

"Good." That's one meal they wouldn't have to cook from scratch. That left time for more important things.

Dani was two steps ahead. She'd also figured out lunch and breakfast recipes.

"How's work going?" He was loath to ask that question, knowing that according to her schedule she shouldn't be sitting with him right now. But he also wasn't about to mess things up for her just because he was feeling selfish.

"It's done—more or less." Dani raised her glass in a mock salute, knocking it gently against his before taking a generous swallow. "That's why I was so tired. I pretty much worked flat out since the last time you were here."

Done. While that thought gave him a great deal of pleasure, he was troubled by the rapid calculations his brain was making. "Do you mean to say you hadn't slept the entire two days?"

"No. I caught a couple of hours yesterday afternoon before dinner. And when you didn't show, I went back to work." That brought up another subject, but Dani let him struggle with that one alone. It was up to Adam how much of his work he shared with her.

"I am sorry, Dani. I meant to come, but things just got complicated." Adam wished for the hundredth time that he could tell her about the case. It wasn't that he didn't trust her. It had nothing to do with that. But even a vague outline of the problem would lead to questions, and those he couldn't answer. Details of that nature were the property of the client, and he had no business sharing them with Dani.

It didn't occur to Adam that even a vague outline might be less trouble than telling her nothing at all.

Dani bit her lip to keep from asking about those complications. He didn't trust her, she realized. That realization impacted her with the force of a physical blow, and she had to concentrate in order to control her breathing. He didn't trust her enough to share his work with her.

It shouldn't have hurt. She even tried to convince herself that it didn't. After all, wasn't she the one who was deliberately refraining from sharing that very same thing with Adam? Trust. Light-years away, she thought. Light-years.

Oblivious to Dani's dismay, Adam dropped the issue of his own work and deftly returned to the subject of her writing.

"Congratulations, Dani," he said, his lips forming a wonderful smile that said he meant it, that he wanted to share her victory. "You should have told me earlier. We could have gone out for a celebration meal." He wondered if she would let him read it, but was afraid of voicing that request. He didn't want to be turned down.

"Well, it's mostly finished. I've still got the mechanics to do." Trying without much success to ignore the resentment at how effectively he was shutting her out of his work, she focused on the book. That, of all things, was now a safe subject. She really didn't have any choice, did she? What could she say? *Trust me enough to share your work, but don't count on me to trust you in return?* Or, even worse, *Trusting is a personal hang-up, but don't worry, we can still sleep together?*

With a level of enthusiasm that was more forced than natural, Dani thrust aside her uncomfortable thoughts and concentrated on telling Adam about the progress she had made. After a few minutes she was surprised to find herself in the middle of telling him about the councilwoman and the Weasel and their parts in the various murders, and giggled at herself. It was terrific having someone to share it with. Leaving him dangling mid-plot, she switched to explaining the routine jobs of proofreading, format and actual printing. "That will take another day or so. I'm not meeting with Agnes until

Tuesday, so I've got plenty of time." She didn't ask if he wanted to help. He probably had to get back to the more important things, like his own business . . . and whatever that encompassed.

"Will I be in the way if I stay?" He didn't want to leave, and there was no reason for it. At least, not yet. He had another "date" with the Channing woman in a couple of days, but until then the surveillance teams would keep an eye on both suspects. Chuck could handle things at the office.

Dani could only smile her answer, pleased with his question, not trusting herself to say the words out loud. Of course, she'd love to have him stay, because anything was better than watching him walk through the door, not knowing if he would ever return. A few days wasn't forever. Commitment was forever. Trust was forever. A few days was precisely that: a few days.

Convinced she was on solid ground, Dani snuggled deeper into the cushions and turned her face into his chest to breathe deeply of his unique scent. He must use mint of some sort in his after-shave, she mused, inhaling with sensuous pleasure.

The arm that was draped over her shoulder tensed, and Dani mewed softly as she was firmly hauled away from her warm nest.

"Does that mean no or yes?"

Dani was quick to realize Adam hadn't been able to see the answer on her face. "Yes," she said, then was shocked to see the animation leave his face and be replaced by a mixture of disappointment and frustration.

Yes, she'd said. Yes, you'll be in the way. How could he make her fall in love with him if she wouldn't let him stay with her? But she was smiling, which either meant she had no idea how much their time together meant to him, or . . .

Adam had a faint suspicion they weren't having the same conversation. He tried out his theory. "Yes . . . what?" Let her explain it.

"Yes, I'd very much like to have you stay and help," she said uncertainly, not having a clue what had brought on the gloom and doom expression. Had she somehow disappointed him?

Perhaps he needed proof. Snagging her handbag from where it lay at the end of the sofa, Dani dug into its depths and finally retrieved her spare key. Handing it to Adam, her eyes questioned his.

It worked. He took the key from her fingers, his light touch sending a message of warmth mingled with an exciting fire that never seemed to lessen. Tucking the key into his pocket, he planted a kiss on her forehead.

A roller coaster had nothing on his emotions, Adam thought irrelevantly. Life with Dani would certainly keep him on his toes. "Good." He gave her a hug to wipe away the confused frown and explained. "I thought you were saying 'Yes, you'll be in the way.' Silly me."

"Yes, silly you." Dani would have to work with Adam on his habit of leaping to conclusions, she decided. Then again, for the most part, it was fun leading him on. She would just have to take care that he was paying attention when they were talking about important stuff. She didn't ever want to hurt him, but a confused Adam was very entertaining.

He gave her another hug, then set her back from him. "I think I'm ready for some sleep. Let's go to bed."

Dani wasn't ready for sleep, but then, Adam's eyes were twinkling again. Perhaps he wasn't so tired after all.

"Where'd all the romance go?" she protested jokingly. "One minute I say you can stay a few days, and the next you're talking about getting some more sleep."

Adam leaned close, his lips hovering at her ear, his warm breath sending shivers down her spine. "Oh, we'll sleep, Dani," he breathed. "Later, after I've touched every corner of your body, after I've tasted what I'm so hungry for, after we're both so exhausted we can't think, then we'll sleep. But I'm not going to begin before we're in your bed because if I do, I'll take you right here, on the sofa, on the coffee table, wherever we fall."

The picture he was painting was incredibly arousing, not that Dani needed any added excitement, and she leaned toward his warmth. But he wasn't there. He was standing beside her, both glasses in his hands. She felt his eyes brand their need onto her, and she burned with the fierceness of his untethered desire. "I don't want to sleep on the sofa, Dani. But if we don't go into the bedroom now, we won't go at all." He moved to take the glasses into the kitchen, then paused, and partially turned back to her. "Please move, Dani. Now."

Personally Dani didn't care where she slept, as long as it was with Adam. And if he was set on the bedroom, then who was she to argue?

"WHERE'S BREAKFAST?" Dani protested when Adam returned from the kitchen with coffee and no food. But that didn't stop her from latching on to a mug of the steaming brew, stopping only to blow lightly on it before taking a careful sip. Too hot, but otherwise quite good. He passed the coffee test.

Dani wondered fleetingly if she, too, was passing those seemingly unimportant tests that made the difference between compatibility and total antipathy, then mentally shrugged her shoulders. She'd know, sooner or later, and worrying about it wouldn't change the outcome. Besides, what difference would it make in the end anyway?

"Too late for breakfast, love," he replied, taking cautious sips from his own cup. "By the time you wash up and get dressed, I'll have lunch on the table." Adam was already finished his own dressing, and wanted to get Dani moving. As he understood it, there was some work to be done on the book.

"Lunch." She mediated about that for a few minutes, then nodded in agreement. "Right. And after lunch, we'll nap." But her eyes flashed another message to Adam.

He groaned, hating to turn down her blatant proposition. Where had all her self-discipline gone? "No, Dani," he said firmly. "Work. Your book. Remember your deadline." She'd said she needed just another day, maybe two.

Dani wasn't in the mood to think about deadlines and schedules when she had other things on her mind. Like the night they'd just spent in each other's arms, exploring every hidden curve, delighting in discovering sensual hot spots. Adam had taught Dani quite a bit last night, mainly about herself. Now she wanted to learn some more, mainly about him.

Adam closed his eyes on her offer, wondering where he'd get the strength to fight her if she really got determined to haul him back into bed. He could still remember the feel of her hands on his body, roaming in sweeping strokes that would encompass all of him, delicately grazing those areas where he was so very sensitive. She delighted in her power to arouse him, laughed when a seemingly careless hand would bring him rigidly hard against her fingers. Her lips had learned his taste, her teeth his texture. Where he'd touched her, she'd touched him, until they were both mindless with wanting.

But now, she had to work. Adam gritted his teeth and evaded the hand that reached out to draw him to her side. He purposefully crossed the room and went into the bathroom where he opened the shower door and turned on the water. Then he returned to the bedroom and lifted a thoroughly delighted Dani from the bed.

"A shower! What a lovely thought," she breathed, wonderfully excited that he had changed his mind. Showering with Adam was definitely a good idea.

Keeping a tight hold on his control, Adam set Dani on her feet and firmly shoved her into the shower, shut the door behind her and leaned his back against it for good measure. He waited for her shrieks to fade, then listened to a remarkable assortment of unladylike obscenities as she searched for and found the temperature controls and adjusted them—in the opposite direction of icy cold! When all the words had stopped, and the steam was rolling out of the open top of the stall, he moved away from his station and entered the bedroom without looking back.

"That's two." Dani spoke the words with quiet determination, knowing they'd reach his ears and have the desired effect. He wasn't going to get away with this.

Adam figured he'd better watch his step, at least until they were married. Maybe then she'd forget to count.

9

"WHERE'D YOU PUT chapter eight?"

Dani ignored him. They were on the final push now, and her powers of concentration were wearing thin. Curled up on the sofa opposite the work area, she did her best to keep her eyes on the papers in her lap and off the man sitting in front of the terminal. It wasn't easy, but it was definitely essential.

Looking at Adam usually prompted an uncontrollable desire to touch him. And *that* wouldn't get the job done—not according to any schedule!

"Dani."

Steeling herself, she raised her head barely enough to see across the room, focusing on the green glow of the computer screen just beyond his left shoulder. "Yes?"

"Chapter eight," he repeated. "I can't find it."

At least it was an easy question, she mused, feeling the full weight of his gaze on her. Anything more difficult would have required more effort than she had to spare. "Over there with two, I think," she replied, and lowered her gaze thankfully. They just might get finished after all!

"What's it doing with two?" Adam asked, not divining the correlation.

Dani gave up the battle, hoping he didn't have anything on his mind besides that blasted chapter. He didn't. She could tell in that first second as she looked up from the typed sheets on her lap and boldly met his questioning stare. He was all business. Unaccountably disappointed, she shot him a look of studied patience tempered with indulgence.

"If you'll remember, chapter two is where I had the first reference to the councilwoman. And chapter eight is where she meets with the detective for the first time. I had to make sure the physical characteristics were consistent." The councilwoman was one of the few characters who had remained unchanged from outline to finished product, and Dani was delighted with her inspiration to use the poisoning scenario when this character killed off the man she had hired to kill the Weasel.

It occurred to her that she still hadn't tested—or retested—the poisoning sequence as performed by the councilwoman, but there was plenty of time. Besides, Dani was confident it would be a snap to execute. There was just the matter of finding a spare hour or so, and with Adam constantly at her side that had been impossible.

"I thought the editor was supposed to spot stuff like that." Adam and Dani had been working with very little time off for breaks for nearly two days, and he was constantly amazed at her attention to detail.

"Yes, an editor is supposed to catch those kinds of mistakes. But if I let something like that get by, then I'm not doing my job. *I'm* writing this book, not the editor. It's my responsibility." Then, with a slightly apologetic note, she added, "The editor stays busy enough double-checking my spelling. Anyway, if any glaring errors managed to get into print, there'd be no end to the number of letters I'd get telling me about them." It never ceased to amaze Dani that letters of criticism were so quick to arrive, while those wonder notes of praise always took longer to reach her.

Adam nodded, imagining for himself the landslide of mail even one error could cause. He went back to his job of sorting and counting. Dani was working with the last chapter now, having left the mechanics of printing to him.

He was convinced a secretary could have done his job in half the time, but was secretly proud of his ability to master the printer and produce the nicely finished copy. It had taken a lot of time, but the hours they'd spent together had been incredibly revealing. Not only were they able to work side by side without bruising egos or fraying delicate nerves, but they enjoyed the process.

The first thing Adam had done was read the entire text. While Dani printed off the hard copy of chapter one, he'd sat in front of the screen flipping through the novel, the green letters dancing in front of his eyes as he followed the intricate plot. He felt so privileged to be the first, and was tremendously proud of Dani's achievement. This was indeed her finest novel to date, and he didn't hesitate to let her know.

That he recognized himself was a foregone conclusion. Both the poisoning in the restaurant and the electrocution in the Jacuzzi were outlined in excruciating detail, the only major changes being the obvious ones. In the book, neither he nor the Weasel had survived. While it didn't necessarily warm his heart to know that Dani had killed him off in his first starring role, he was privately flattered with her sinister, yet sensuous portrayal of his character.

And one scene she'd included between his character and the councilwoman was a fantasy he intended to bring to life.

Adam worked alongside Dani, doing whatever he was instructed to do. They chatted easily during their breaks, and Adam found out more about her family in Montana. There was a lot to learn, he soon discovered.

It began innocently enough. Just another simple discussion with Dani. He should have known better. They had been talking about the Thanksgiving holidays, and he remembered that she had spoken with her mother about spending that time in Montana. Adam was working on an invitation for himself.

"Have you decided if you'll go yet?" he asked innocently, prodding her into one further intimacy. Spending a holiday with family would lend a permanence to their relationship, and the idea of it might force her to look beyond the next few days or weeks.

Dani just shook her head, incapable of thinking that far ahead. As it was, she felt her control over her emotions slipping away with each hour Adam spent in her home. It was only supposed to be a few days, she knew, but as the time passed, she began to dread his leaving.

She figured the end could only be another day or two in the offing, and now he was talking about a time that was over a month away. She couldn't bring herself to consider the future. Plans required commitment, perhaps only a token sign of obligation, but a certain level of trust nevertheless.

She hoped it would be easier when he went back to his own place. Without his constant attention, the control she so desperately sought would come more easily.

"Your mother mentioned six brothers." Imagining six masculine versions of Dani, aged about eight to eighteen, Adam was looking forward to meeting them. Being the eldest child in his family, he assumed Dani was also the first of the seven children. It was a rash assumption, built upon his own frustrated desire to have a kid brother.

"Are all of them still in school?" He figured the Thanksgiving holiday would be a good time to meet them all, and he pictured a happy family scene, the boys and men gathered around the television, watching college football while the two women flitted back and forth between the kitchen and dining room, preparing the traditional feast.

"School?" Dani knit her brows, trying to remember how old she'd been when Craig, the youngest of her brothers, had graduated from college. About two years before her own graduation, she recalled. "No. They're not in school."

"None of them?"

"Nope."

"They've just finished then," he concluded. He revised the happy picture in his head, finding himself just as pleased with the alternative. This time, instead of men and boys gathered around the television, there were just men. Adam, Danielle's father, and an assortment of young men, probably all still in their twenties. That still worked. The only difference was they were slightly larger than in the last scene, the fourteen-year-old now a fully developed twenty-one. Dani and her mother hadn't changed a bit in this updated scene—they were still preparing the lavish feast.

Dani was beginning to see he had a misconception about her family. This might be fun, she thought. "Adam, I'm not sure how to break this to you, but they're all big brothers."

"Big as in older or big as in large?"

"Both." She smiled, delivering the blow cleanly.

No wonder Beatrice Courtland had mentioned Dani's brothers. Adam saw it all clearly now. What he'd earlier appreciated as a mother's subtle warning was in fact a very real threat. Six large brothers to protect their little sister.

Good thing she didn't need it.

"How big?" he asked. It wouldn't hurt to find out now—just in case. While Adam knew they were headed toward a very *married* future together, Dani was still unaware of this. And if Dani didn't know, it only stood to reason her six brothers also didn't know. He could easily imagine a misunderstanding arising about their living arrangement, and six protective brothers was no joke.

"Bigger than you." Dani stretched that a bit. It was fun watching Adam sweat. Only half of them were bigger. The other three were about the same size.

"Bigger than me?" Adam wasn't considered a small man, not by any stretch of the imagination.

"Yup."

"Oh." He wondered if she'd agree to a wedding the next weekend. That sounded like the safest bet. The thought of their imminent wedding brought the smile back to his face, and he made plans to let Dani in on the secret the minute she turned the novel over to Agnes.

Just a few more days.

Dani watched his confidence return, shaken but not diminished, and wondered what had bolstered his courage. No matter. She'd had her fun, but she decided to let him stew a bit before extending the holiday invitation he so obviously wanted. Why he wanted to go was a complete mystery to Dani, but she was secretly delighted he wanted to meet her family. Even if it meant putting her own emotions through the wringer, she thought she could handle it.

It suddenly didn't make sense to view their relationship as a temporary thing. Looking ahead to a holiday, planning to do things together... these were no more threatening than the intimacies they had already shared. Time could only be her enemy if she let it. She just had to keep everything in perspective, to control that tendency to think of Adam as a permanent fixture in her life.

She could do it. Of course she could.

Meanwhile, there was plenty of time before Thanksgiving. She wanted to see how blatant Adam could get with his hints.

Another thought occurred to him. "I'll bet you and your mom have a great time on Thanksgiving!" he said, unable to keep the hopeful note out of his voice. Not only was he angling for an invitation, but his scene of domestic bliss—now severely altered by the unexpected size of the male contingent—couldn't be complete without a well-prepared feast.

Dani merely raised an eyebrow, not having the faintest idea what he was getting at now. Besides the obvious hint, that is.

"The food," he prompted, settling back against the sofa cushions, picturing Dani with an apron on that matched her green eyes. That was nice. "It must be a challenge cooking for so many men."

"The food?" Dani was catching on. Slowly. But she had begun to figure out what he was getting at. He thought Dani and her mother cooked the Thanksgiving meal. What a joke!

"If I didn't know you better, I'd say that was a chauvinistic remark." Let him stew a little. He deserved it.

"Dani, I didn't mean . . ." he began, flustered that his picture of domestic bliss was falling apart around his ears. Then he replayed his words back in his head, and saw how she could misinterpret what he had said. Dropping his chin to rest in abject misery on his chest, Adam pondered how he was going to talk his way out of this mess and still get invited for the Thanksgiving holidays. If he had to, he would offer to help cook.

"Of course, you didn't," she agreed, patting him on the hand with tolerant conviction. "But it sure sounded like it."

"You see, I have this picture in my head of your family, and every time you say something, I have to change the picture." Weak, but then sometimes the truth seems that way.

Dani nodded her head in agreement. She knew what it was like to have preconceived notions of how things were supposed to be, and then have them end up quite differently. That first night at the restaurant, when the scenario for poisoning the Weasel had fallen apart, was a prime example.

"Dad and the boys cook," she said.

"Who watches football?"

"We all do. Dad took over cooking the Thanksgiving meal about the time they started televising football games nonstop on that holiday," she said, and then explained about her mother's addiction to college football, making her father's cooking seem more a self-defense than the reflection of any gentlemanly instinct. Left to Beatrice Courtland, the meal never got finished. "When he first made the boys help, they were always popping into the sitting room to watch the game and things sometimes got burned. So now he rents another TV set for the kitchen and they all watch while they cook."

"Does your mom help?"

"Are you kidding?" she exclaimed, laughing outright at his suggestion. "She knows when she's got a good thing going."

Adam quit while he was still ahead. . . . Well, ahead wasn't exactly where he was, but it was better than nowhere.

And he still didn't have an invitation. But he took heart. She'd *have* to take him if they were married!

ADAM DIDN'T CONFINE himself to the job of clerk and printer. He also had some minor suggestions to offer about the novel, not all of which were accepted graciously.

"Don't be silly, Adam. Of course he can take a bath in chapter five." They were talking about the detective, and Dani was humoring him. Everyone was a critic.

"No, he can't. Not in chapter five, not in chapter eight." It was a small discrepancy, but Adam held his ground.

Dani smothered her irritation, hoping this was not the pattern of the days to come. She hadn't asked for him to make editorial comments, but she firmly held on to her good humor. After his first reading, the praise he'd heaped upon her and, therefore, the book had been comforting indeed. "Why?" Anything to get this out of the way so she could go back to her own final checking.

"He doesn't have a bathtub." An obvious answer, he thought.

"Oh." Dani screwed up her forehead, then grabbed for chapter four. It was on the desk under chapters six and seven. She flipped rapidly through the pages until she found the description of the detective's apartment, then sighed in resignation. There it was, in her own words. "He came out of the shower stall, the door swinging open to crash as it always did against the toilet stool, leaving just enough room to squeeze by the sink as he fought his way out of the slippery cubicle." No bath, she agreed. The impression she had wanted to leave with the reader was one of scant space, minimum convenience, totally bereft of luxury.

"You win," she said, then tossed four aside after making a note on the pad at her side. Without another glance at Adam, she continued reading the chapter in her lap. Maybe he'd get the hint and leave well enough alone.

Luckily for Adam, he only found two other minor points worth mentioning.

"YOU'RE JOKING, of course."

"Nope."

Dani stood in the middle of the living room, *Adam's* living room, hands on her hips and an expression of disbelief on her face.

"Pull the other one, Adam!" she joked, wondering why he had brought her here. They were supposed to be going to his apartment to pick up some clothes. The light dawned. "I'll bet this is just a place your company keeps for secret meetings and stuff." Adam had a bizarre sense of humor.

He grinned sheepishly, and agreed. "Yeah, we sometimes use it for that kind of 'stuff.' But the rest of the time, it's my apartment."

Dani just shook her head in amazement, incapable of believing anyone could live in a place without nesting, branding it with their own personality, turning a dwelling into a home. She was speechless.

"I'll, er, just grab some clothes," he muttered, escaping down a little hallway that led off the kitchen. It was worse than he had figured, and he profoundly regretted bringing her here.

"And I thought the living room was bad!"

Adam whipped his head around to discover Dani had followed him into his bedroom. Following her stare, he had to admit she wasn't far off base. At least the living room had some extra pieces of furniture. The nightstand, lamp and bed that comprised the entire contents of this room gave it a rather Spartan look...and he knew he was being kind with his description.

To Dani it was sterile. Not just this room but the whole apartment, which was no more than a group of rooms arranged in a collective unit to provide a convenient base for an occasional visitor. It reflected absolutely nothing of the personality of the man who paid real dollars to maintain the address.

"No pictures of your family. No plants. Not even a stain on the carpet with a wild story behind it." She returned to the living room, arms hugging her waist and a scowl on her lips.

"I just moved here," he offered, zipping his bag closed as he followed Dani down the short hallway.

"When?" she asked suspiciously.

"Last year?" So much for good excuses.

She shook her head, trailing her gaze over the neatly organized bookshelves, immaculate end tables and new-looking furniture. "A year, and this place still looks like a motel."

"I haven't been home much."

"No kidding?" she retorted, wondering with sudden fury how many other women had provided him with a place to stay during that year. It was the only explanation. He really *didn't* live here. Now, for example, he was living with Dani, probably hoping to stretch the couple of days to a month or more.

Over my dead body, she resolved. Not for anything was Dani about to provide a convenient "home away from home" for Adam. Not for any man!

"I traveled a lot last year. I haven't had time to do much with this place." Adam was getting just a little irritated at Dani's critical attitude. He *had* been busy. Besides, this was only a temporary place. He'd been looking for a house up toward the mountains for several months now, and the more he'd looked, the less he'd been inclined to do anything here.

"I'll bet you tell that to all your women," she muttered under her breath.

"You're wrong, Dani."

Snapping her head up so fast she could hear the pop of an unsuspecting joint, Dani realized he had heard her. The teasing light was gone from his eyes, and they now flashed a warning that was neither gentle nor subtle. Speechless with the dramatic change in his mood, she noted the rigid set of his jaw, the clenched fists at his side.

"You're wrong to judge my home by your own standards. Just because your ivory tower is tailored to indulge your every whim doesn't mean the rest of the world has time for such nonsense," he said, spitting the words out between clenched teeth. Adam was angry, frustrated, and not a little disappointed. Dani had let him down. And what was that nonsense about other women?

Shocked at the attack, Dani blanched at the truth behind his accusation. She *had* constructed a shelter where she could retreat from the world, rendering herself immune from life's uncertain treatment. But what did that have to do with what she was thinking? Nothing. But then, perhaps it was better if Adam didn't guess the real reason behind her disbelief. He would probably jump to the conclusion that she was jealous. She wasn't, of course. And if Adam wanted to maintain the pretense that he really lived here, that was his business.

As far as Dani was concerned, after a few days were up, they would go back to conducting their affair from separate dwellings. *Affair?* She silently mouthed the word, and it left a bitter taste on her lips. Is that what she really wanted with Adam?

"I'm not saying my life-style is none of your business," he continued in measured tones. "I'm merely pointing out that jumping to conclusions won't get us anywhere."

"You're right, of course," she said quietly. About jumping to conclusions, that is. That didn't mean she was wrong, just that there was insufficient evidence. Dani still chafed at the idea that she was merely the most recent of a long line of accommodating women. The most recent, not the last.

Adam caught the flicker of pain that crossed her face. Was he somehow missing the point? If he hadn't known better, he would have sworn that Dani was jealous!

That was it! He suppressed any outward signs of the relief that surged through him. Jealousy was only possible if one felt possessive toward another. And if Dani felt possession, love might be just around the corner.

"I'm surprised at you, Dani. Don't you know you're the only woman in my life?" Moving toward her with unhurried steps, Adam hunkered down beside her, his eyes now level with her own. "Somehow, I thought you had begun to trust me."

"Trust you?" Shaking her head, Dani couldn't keep it inside. Her entire body trembling with the inner battles she fought, she asked, "Why should I trust you? I hardly know you."

"Don't you know that I want you, that I need you? You have to know you're special, love," he breathed, closing the distance between them to draw his tongue along her tender lips. She moved her head, following his mouth, opening her lips to his. Trust aside, Dani needed him. Adam could use that, build on it.

It was a beginning. For now, he would just try to hold her with the physical side of their relationship. Later, after the pressure of her book was relieved, they would talk. It might not solve anything, not immediately, but it would be a step in the right direction. If he could bring her fears into the open, they could deal with them together. Suddenly, Adam found he had resources of patience he had never before imagined. There was nothing tentative about the tongue that thrust deep inside Dani's mouth. It was the first parry in a fight Adam was determined to win.

He still wanted her, Dani silently rejoiced, opening her mouth wide under the urgent pressure of Adam's demanding tongue. He wanted her, and nothing else seemed to matter. Disagreements aside, Adam was drawing her into a vortex of pleasure and ecstasy that overrode her control and made mockery of her doubts.

How could she not love the man who sent her to such heights? And if she loved him, how could she not trust him? It was something not even Dani understood.

And for the moment, she ceased to care. With trembling fingers she drew him closer to her mouth as Dani buried herself in the exquisite sensations of Adam's lovemaking.

"IT'S ALMOST LUNCHTIME," he remarked as he retrieved a page which had fallen to the floor, inserting it in its proper place once he ascertained it was unblemished. Not that his hints about food would do any good. It usually took a good hour to tear Dani away from her work.

"Be quiet. I'm nearly done." She didn't even lift her eyes from the pages, silently turning them one by one. Then, to his total amazement, she rose, thrusting the sheaf of papers into his hands. "Your turn," she said with a smile. "I'll cook something special."

"You're done?" He couldn't believe his luck. It was barely noon, and he wouldn't have to leave until early evening. A quick meeting with Chuck at his apartment while he changed clothes, then the date with the Channing woman. With luck, he could be back by midnight.

He smiled, then leered.

Dani caught the look, but pretended she was too much of a lady to catch his meaning. Flicking an imaginary piece of lint from her shirt, she ignored him totally and left the room.

Adam dove into the chair and started up the printer. Time was wasting.

THE SOMETHING SPECIAL she managed to throw together consisted of an amazing assortment of fresh vegetables, lightly stir-fried and served with tender medallions of pork cooked in a pineapple sauce. She'd obviously made a run to the store for supplies. Adam had heard her go out the door, but hadn't even looked up from his own work.

"I like this," he said between mouthfuls. "A lot." He was glad to notice she'd made enough for leftovers. He really hated to fight over food.

"Of course you do," Dani agreed. "You like everything I cook." She also liked the meal, but her appetite for a greasy hamburger and fries was almost overwhelming. Maybe later Adam would take a nap and she'd be able to slip out for a run and head over toward fast-food row, conveniently located just six blocks from her house. When she'd gone to the store for groceries earlier, she had been too rushed to sneak by and pick up a burger. And Adam might have noticed the giveaway traces of pickles and onions on her breath.

When the dishes were done, it was just past two o'clock. They had been up since dawn, working on the book. But that was finished now, and Adam had some serious plans on his mind as he led Dani to the nearby sofa.

Dani wasn't averse to letting Adam nibble on her neck, stretching like a cat as she offered every inch for his caress. Of course, she had her own plans for the afternoon. A run to smooth out the kinks followed by a movie sounded about right. She had been more or less shut up in this house for over a week, not counting the trips to Adam's apartment and the store, and she needed a good dose of crowds and noise. And the plants needed moving, she knew, grateful that Adam would be here to help. She really hated lugging them up and down the stairs. But ten minutes on the sofa with Adam weren't out of order.

Unfortunately Myra was early.

First, the doorbell rang. Adam was too involved in his thorough investigation of Dani's neck to do much about it. But Dani knew better. Myra had her own key.

Dani reluctantly put some distance between her neck and Adam's hungry lips, scooting to the end of the sofa as she dragged her fingers through the thick strands of honey-blond hair.

"That's Myra."

Adam was still in shock from Dani's inexplicable withdrawal. He reached across the cushions, determined to drag her back into his arms. This wasn't going at all the way he'd planned.

But Dani evaded his grasp. She didn't think she'd be able to pull away a second time, and it would be just her luck to have Myra start cleaning the upstairs first.

Adam gave up trying to corral Dani, and briefly considered resorting to pouting, but he figured she probably wouldn't respond to that tactic. His mind sorted through various options even as he expressed curiosity about the doorbell. "What's a Myra?"

"My cleaning lady," Dani said, then moved to open the door leading to the downstairs. "I called her earlier to let her know I was finished with the book."

Adam barely suppressed a sudden urge to pout in earnest. "Why did you have to call her today?" he asked, his own plans for the afternoon crashing about his ears.

"This place is a mess," Dani threw over her shoulder, then added, "and I'm nearly out of clean clothes." Myra was familiar with Dani's work habits, and they'd come to a mutual agreement several years ago that she would take a holiday during Dani's peak work periods, then come in and clear out the mess all in one swoop. This strategy worked well, and Dani always marked the true finish of her book when the house was once again sparkling clean and livable. Handing the manuscript over to her agent was a mere formality in the face of this other ritual.

The phone rang before Adam could follow her down the stairs and he went to answer it, reason telling him Dani's mother certainly wouldn't be calling again so soon. He was right. It was Chuck.

Adam spoke briefly with him, stoically accepting the fact that he was needed at the office. He replaced the receiver and checked his watch. He had time to shower and change before going to meet Chuck. He headed into the bathroom, pulling clean clothes out of the closet on his way. It was a good thing he'd had a chance to run over to his own apartment the previous day, he thought. Even then, his supply of clothes was dwindling, and he needed to get some laundry done. Adam wondered how Myra would feel about an increased laundry load.

He was out of the shower and dressed before Dani returned from the first floor.

"Where are you going?" she asked, noting the fresh clothes. "I thought you didn't have to leave until later." Maybe he was uncomfortable having Myra wandering around. More likely, he was a mind reader and was getting out before he could get sucked into manhandling the plants.

Adam pulled on a sports jacket and crossed to give Dani a reassuring hug. "Chuck needs me at the office, love," he said with more than a touch of disappointment. "I've got to go earlier than I'd planned." He went on to remind her he wouldn't be returning until late, sometime after dinner.

Their couple of days were over, but he hadn't made any moves to return to his own place. And for the life of her, Dani couldn't bring herself to suggest it. Another day, she resolved. Just one more day. Then they would have to put some physical distance between them. Otherwise, things were going to get out of control.

Dani couldn't bring herself to admit that it was already too late.

"Fine," she said firmly, standing on her toes to plant a chaste kiss on his cheek. "With Myra in the house, you'd just be in the way." There, she thought, that should put him in his place.

Adam grinned at her not-so-subtle hint, kissed her hard on the mouth to let her know she wasn't fooling him one bit and quickly left. Dani was trying, he thought. She didn't want him to leave, but she had hidden her own feelings and practically pushed him out the door. At least she wasn't worried about him anymore.

When he returned, they'd have that talk he had planned—the one about trust. And love. The book was finished, and she couldn't use that to evade the issue. Adam's heart thumped at an irregular pace, then steadied. It wouldn't help to worry about the outcome. It had to be done. Without it, they were going nowhere.

Dani waited until she heard the front door slam shut before she let her fists clench and her eyes squeeze shut. He'd come back. Unless he ran into trouble and got hurt. Dani nudged that frightening thought aside, determined to quell the irrational fear that was born that second he had shut the door. She'd have to do something about that, she knew. If . . . when . . . he came back, she would have to tell him that she couldn't live that way.

But for how long could she count on Adam's returning?

It was senseless to worry about something she couldn't control, she chided herself, crossing to open a drawer and pull out her running shorts and top. She decided to take the run she'd promised herself and indulge in a greasy hamburger. The movie still sounded like a good idea, and she made a note to check the paper for show times.

She finished dressing and tugged on her tennis shoes before heading down the stairs. Shouting to Myra that she was leaving, Dani slipped out of the front door and headed for the park.

10

IT TOOK DANI over an hour to shift and "shower" all the plants. Coming on top of the long run she'd taken, the additional exercise left her winded. Draped crossways on one of the deeply cushioned armchairs, she contemplated the stillness that surrounded her.

It was Adam's fault, Dani knew. The silence had never bothered her before. In just the few days since they'd met, Adam had managed to completely alter the atmosphere of her home. Now, instead of being simply alone, she was lonely in his absence.

And bored. That had never happened to her before. But it was better than worrying—something she was trying hard to avoid!

Shaking off the unaccustomed mood, Dani investigated the possibilities of self-entertainment. Reading was ruled out in favor of an especially graphic horror movie on television, and she sprawled on the carpet in front of the color set in the living room. But even the disgusting antics of a man-eating slug failed to keep her attention, and she found her eyes wandering to the clock with increasing frequency.

The inspiration, when it finally came, galvanized Dani into a flurry of preparations. Rushing to her closet, she selected a simple knee-length black dress with long sleeves and a boat neckline. While not precisely eye-catching, it was a subtle statement of neutrality. She wanted to blend in without feeling dumpy. Dani pulled on the dress and twisted a couple of strings of beads around her neck for a spot of color. Tossing the necessary equipment into a matching purse, she paused only to pull on a pair of heels before hurrying out the door.

She had almost forgotten about the last murder in her book, and that would never do. Tonight was probably her last chance!

Pointing her car in the direction of a nearby singles bar, Dani mentally rehearsed the scene. Snuggle up to the bar next to the servers' station, pour the contents of the vial into any drink, and get out. Fast. No need to get technical. She just wanted to prove she could perform that one step without getting caught. The details, like whom she was poisoning, didn't concern her. Dani was satisfied that she'd successfully accomplished that part before, and she didn't have time for a repeat performance.

It had to be quick, she told herself. She wanted to be home before Adam returned.

Ten minutes later, she confidently pushed the heavy wood door and entered the bar. Sweeping her eyes around the smoke-filled room, she was disturbed to find it was considerably more crowded than she had expected. The popular watering hole was jammed with wall to wall people, the long bar totally obscured by a throng of eager singles. But perhaps that would work in her favor, she mused. Escaping into a crowd was a classic getaway technique.

Moving slowly down the length of the bar, Dani kept her eyes peeled for a waitress. Eventually two young women dressed alike in what had to be uniforms elbowed their way into the center of the crowd, disappearing as they passed through the first layer. Dani slowly worked her way in their direction, pausing when she lost sight of them. She waited patiently and was soon rewarded when one reappeared, balancing a tray that was laden with a variety of drinks.

She had found the source. Now, she just had to get close to it.

Dani took a deep breath for courage, then plunged into the crowd. It was an extremely physical undertaking, not so much in the sense of being difficult, but rather like playing a game of wiggle and pass! Making intimate contact with the men and women who surrounded her was unavoidable, and Dani tried not to flinch at the occasional elbow she encountered.

But that was the least of her worries! With an overabundance of men in the mob, Dani soon found herself blushing at the whispered suggestions and innuendoes directed at her. If she hadn't been alone, it probably wouldn't have happened. But a single woman was fair game in these bars, and it was expected that if she came alone, then she could take care of herself. And as Dani had persistently avoided these places since her days at college, she didn't have much practice in fending off unwanted propositions.

Holding onto a tight smile, Dani pretended to ignore all comments, dodging without much success a man who was making a game out of blocking her way. She resisted the temptation to plant her heel on his foot, figuring that with her current run of bad luck she'd miss and cripple the wrong man, and she couldn't afford to draw attention to herself. Just as she was getting set to duck under his elbow, the waitress plowed her way past. Dani quickly followed in her wake before the sea of humanity closed in the gap, and found herself tightly pinned between a high stool—occupied—and the servers' station.

She didn't even hear the shout of outrage as her neat move caused her erstwhile blocker to dump the contents of his glass down the front of his shirt.

Unfortunately for Dani there was no way on earth she could maneuver the vial out of her purse from her present position. She was too short, and the bar was high. Reviewing her options, Dani figured she had two alternatives. She could either attempt to coax the heavy-set man into giving up his stool, or give up now. A calculating glance at the man didn't reassure her, but Dani was a fighter, and this was her last chance to perform the deed. Squaring her shoulders, she decided it was worth a try.

Later, she concluded she must have been out of her mind.

"Excuse me?" Dani used her sweetest voice, and threw in a pair of batting eyelashes for good measure.

He didn't turn around.

Dani cleared her throat, trying again, a few decibels louder this time. "Er, excuse me!"

Still nothing. Dani resorted to a tactile approach. Laying her hand on the rough linen plaid that stretched tightly across his full-backer shoulders, Dani communicated with a modified yell. *"Excuse me!"*

It worked. Turning as much as the crowds would allow, the occupant of the stool directed an interested stare at Dani.

Gulping, Dani removed her hand. She should have been warned by the sheer size of the man. Big and Brawny might have been two of his Christian names. But no, Dani had been so desperate to conclude the last stages of her murder that she'd ignored the little voice inside that warned of her impending doom.

And, despite the ball of nervous tension that lodged itself deep in her belly, she continued to ignore the niggling sense of unease. She had his attention. Now, all she had to do was work that to her advantage. *Just like you worked the crowd to your advantage*, the voice chided her, but Dani ignored it.

"Would you take ten bucks for that chair?" she asked, batting her eyelids in a rhythm that matched her racing heartbeat. Somehow, she was willing to bet this wasn't going to turn out to be one of her better plans.

She would have won.

"You'll give me ten bucks for what?" he asked, totally oblivious to anything but the rise and fall of her breasts under the crepe wool dress. Dani cringed at his blatant stare, wishing she had stayed at home. *Ogle*. Dani had never used the word before, but it suddenly gained definition and a sordid vitality. *Leer* was too polite a term for the way he was staring at her.

This was *not* working out as planned.

"For your chair. Stool." When he didn't respond, she phrased it as simply as possible, "A place to sit."

A broad smile broke his uncomfortable gaze, and Dani congratulated herself for making a genuine breakthrough.

That was before Big and Brawny reached down with his massive paws to drag her onto his lap.

"Ayy—eek—lemme down!" she sputtered, using her elbows for punctuation until he managed to get a colossal arm around her waist. The puny jabs weren't making any impression on him, but Dani wasn't about to give up. Besides, she was attracting a considerable amount of attention from the surrounding crowd.

Ducking the furiously twisting limbs, Big and Brawny let out a bellow of intimidating proportions. "But you said you wanted a place to sit!" he roared, silencing the babble around them. Their audience was suddenly spellbound, captivated by the spectacle of a wrestling match between the two most unmatched opponents in the bar.

Dani was equal to the occasion, and raised her voice to heights that matched her extraordinary level of indignation. "You ignorant buffalo!" she shrieked. "I offered to buy your chair, not rent your lap!"

Clearly, Big and Brawny was not amused at being called a buffalo. Or maybe it was the *ignorant* that provoked him. Either way, he let out another roar, the magnitude of which was quantum leaps ahead of his earlier bellows.

Dani didn't have the sense to be frightened. Rather, she figured he probably wouldn't murder her in front of all these witnesses. Instead, she concentrated on wiggling and punching her way out of his grasp before the heavies arrived to break it up.

In her experience, a confrontation with the heavies, or bouncers as some would call them, inevitably concluded with Dani in jail. Again. And the last thing Dani wanted was to spend the night in the local lockup.

In the end, she didn't have much choice.

BY THE TIME Adam arrived to collect Stephanie at her apartment, he was thirty minutes late. And when she didn't bitch about it, he knew his number was up. Stephanie had more in mind tonight than dinner, and it wasn't dancing!

Adam nearly turned tail. Surely Baxter didn't expect him to throw personal scruples to the four winds? But Adam didn't run, managing instead a bleak smile of apology for his tardiness.

He could handle her. One way or the other, he would find a way to thwart her lascivious plans. *Lascivious*. That wasn't a word he normally associated with women. *Sensual, erotic, sexy . . .*

But Stephanie Channing wasn't any of those. Not to Adam.

Sensual, erotic and *sexy* described Dani. Along with *loving, tender* and *gentle*. Not to mention *intelligent, perceptive* and *clever*.

None of which would get him through the evening with Stephanie.

Fronting his best smile, Adam ushered her into his car. At least she hadn't insisted on having a drink at her apartment. Things might have gotten tense there. In a public restaurant, Adam figured his chances of escaping unscathed were better.

Driving the few blocks to the restaurant, Adam congratulated himself on his choice. There was no dance floor, just piped-in music that one ignored for the most part.

But Stephanie would probably demand to be taken dancing. Adam had also blocked that avenue. He sported a fake limp in his right—or was that his left?—leg, a perfect excuse to avoid an unwanted intimacy.

Intimacy. That was a concept he shared with Dani. Certainly not this Channing woman.

They were just a few blocks from the restaurant when he noticed the disturbance in front of a neighborhood singles joint. The citizens of Denver were taking advantage of the lull in traffic, rubber-necking to their hearts content, so Adam was forced to slow his own pace.

There had evidently been a scuffle inside, and it was now occupying a large part of the sidewalk. Cheered on by a hoard of howling supporters, the combatants were being hauled away by the cops. Adam grinned, amused with the unequivocal support the crowd was lending to one of the principals in the scrimmage. A flash of blond hair halted the even beat of his heart, but he ignored the untimely reminder of Dani.

She was waiting for him, back in the house he was learning to call home. And he would go to her. Soon, after this interminable evening was finished. They would talk. And hopefully her doubts would surface to a level where he could dispose of them.

In the meantime he needed every tiny fragment of his concentration to keep Stephanie Channing interested . . . and at arm's length!

WHEN THE BATTERY-OPERATED mechanism in his pocket beeped its steady message, Adam wasn't merely relieved. He was elated.

As he had predicted, events had progressed from bad to worse. Stephanie wanted action, of the sexual sort, and the signals she sent him were as blatant as they were unavoidable. Adam had the choice of taking her dancing, which he couldn't, or taking her to bed, which he wouldn't. Actually, dancing was of negligible importance. She meant to get him into her bed, and it was crystal clear to Adam that she would take no excuses.

By excluding himself from either denouement, he would alienate Stephanie Channing and sacrifice the agency's best contact with their prime suspect.

Adam was a formidable opponent, but he was up the creek without a paddle. There was no way he'd comply with her desires, but he couldn't figure a way out of it.

On the down side, it meant the end of easy contact with Channing.

On the up side, Adam wouldn't have to leave Dani so often. Especially not now, a time they needed together, the beginning of the rest of their lives.

But when the beeper sounded, it was a symphony in his ears. Excusing himself from the leech he'd shared dinner with, Adam practically ran to the telephone. He was halfway there before he remembered the limp.

It wasn't Chuck, as he'd expected. Rather, it *was* Chuck, but with a message from Dani.

She was looking for someone to bail her out of jail.

Chuck's first question was, "Who's Dani?" But he didn't really need to ask. Adam had been spending his free time somewhere, and Chuck had no doubt figured that somewhere was with Dani.

His second question was whether Adam had sufficient cash to bail her out. Apparently she'd chalked up enough charges to warrant a small fortune.

DANI LET HERSELF INTO the house with her key, leaving the door open for Adam. It wouldn't have helped to lock it behind her—even if she'd wanted to. Even if she hadn't already given him a key, Adam knew how to get in without the benefit of conventional utensils.

In the hour since he'd arrived at the jail, he hadn't expressed any surprise. Or anger.

But Dani was suspicious of the amusement he was trying—and failing!—to hide. She knew him better than he thought, better than *she* had thought. And he was *laughing* at her!

By taking the stairs two at a time, she managed to flip on all the lights, toss her coat into the corner and jump up to perch on the kitchen counter before he was in the front door. This was important. If he was going to lecture her, he would do it from a position of disadvantage.

She'd had a lot of experience at being on the receiving end of lectures. Agnes had talked herself blue on multiple occasions.

But the difference with Agnes was that her agent secretly supported Dani's adventures in the name of research.

Dani didn't figure Adam would share the same point of view.

He had been silent during the entire procedure which included counting out the big bucks and promising the authorities that Dani wouldn't get into more trouble before her trial. He'd heard the whole story from the dozen or so witnesses who had crowded into the station in support of Dani.

They had actually left the bar and followed her to the station to plead her case! Adam's mind was boggled by the pro-Dani sentiment that had brought them there. Unfortunately the large fines she had incurred were more than their collective wallets could support, and she had found herself seeking outside assistance.

The charges of disturbing the peace, assault and inciting to riot weren't cheap in any city, and Denver was tougher than most.

Agnes, apparently, had made herself unavailable. Adam knew Dani was upset about having to call him, but the threatened time in jail had forced her hand. Calling him had not only been her last resort, it had been her only recourse. That is, short of calling her mother.

Adam was pretty sure she wouldn't have done that.

Perhaps, after they were married, he'd tell her about the female piranha she'd saved him from.

In the meantime, she was expecting a lecture. He didn't want to disappoint her. Her position was clear. Seated defiantly on the counter, she was ready and willing to defend each and every charge.

"Inciting to riot, Dani?" he probed gently, trying to keep a straight face. That was a new one for the file. Along with assault. She'd never been charged with that before.

"It was a slow night," she shrugged, not at all sure where she stood. Any other man would have walked away in horror. It almost seemed as though Adam was teasing her. "Sorry to pull you away from your big investigation," she said in that offhand way that meant she was still upset at not knowing what she might have interrupted.

The remark was on the nasty side, but Adam forgave her that. If he didn't tell her anything, did he deserve any better?

Yes, he decided. It was his money that was keeping her on the comfortable side of bars and regimentation. He deserved to hear some sort of an explanation.

Besides, he hadn't had a good laugh since Chuck had beeped him at the restaurant. And after he returned to face Stephanie at their table, it had been nearly impossible to hide his grin—especially when he was trying to act contrite for having to end their evening together. But he had somehow managed to sound appropriately frustrated by the "business" that called him away, and had loaded her into a taxi before she could protest more vehemently.

Now, picking his way carefully through the defensive barbs Dani had fixed at her most vulnerable points, Adam tried another approach. "If I promise not to bicker about it, will you tell me why you challenged the biggest man this side of Redwood, California?"

Dani grinned. It was going to be okay.

Unless, of course, Big and Brawny pressed charges.

She didn't know why, but his meaning was clear. Adam didn't blame her for the fiasco at the bar.

It suddenly became more important to tell him something totally unrelated. "I missed you."

Adam smiled in return. "I missed you, too."

"Can it wait until tomorrow?" she asked. It had been a long night, and there were other things on her mind.

"Yeah," he said, shucking his jacket in an easy movement. "It can wait." After all, he'd waited to hear about the vagrancy thing for what seemed like ages. Her newest escapade wouldn't suffer for the telling if they put it off a few hours.

He closed the distance between them, reaching up to lift Dani from her perch. Carefully he held Dani against him, lowering her in a motion that suspended all thought. The tension that claimed his body had nothing to do with investigations and jails and bail money.

This was Dani at her best. Excited and loving and passionate.

All Adam wanted to do was please her. And, in so doing, he pleased himself.

Pleased. What a tame word.

"I JUST REMEMBERED. I was supposed to call Agnes this morning."

"Why?"

Dani mumbled something totally unintelligible, tossing in words like *publisher* and *royalties* and *deadlines*. With any luck, he'd be too tired to pursue it, although the sounds of easily controlled breathing from her running partner didn't allude to the least bit of weariness. He was either in terrific shape and was suffering no ill effects whatsoever after their late-night snack, or, more likely, was keeping up out of sheer male stubbornness. The course Dani set that morning had been vigorous and fast, but not too vigorous, not too fast. That would have been asking for trouble.

For her own part, Dani was ready to fade into the grassy running path. They'd celebrated the finish of her novel—not to mention her timely release from jail—late into the night, with an unlikely assortment of leftovers from the freezer that included lasagne, her special cheese and onion enchiladas and chicken satay. And Kirin, naturally.

On top of the treats she had managed to sneak the day before, it went without saying that her stomach needed a fix of normal, unspiced food that would both satisfy her awakening appetite and appease her craving for sugar.

Doughnuts.

Dani figured a small quantity from the shop on fast-food row would take care of her problem. Unfortunately there was a complication keeping pace with her, and she had to ditch him before she could cut back to her ultimate goal.

"Call her later." Adam needed to get another three miles—minimum!—under his belt if he was going to make that side trip he was planning on later. After eating his share of that bizarre variety of food Dani had pulled out of her bottomless freezer, he felt like his stomach was going to drop out. Rich, ethnic food was wonderful, but although the "rich" part was clotting his veins, he had an uncontrollable urge for a contrast . . . a foil . . . a hamburger! Or, considering the hour, a few doughnuts would do the trick.

It seemed to Adam that one category balanced the other, made one appreciate each for what they were. While Dani was a marvelous cook, it was easier to enjoy her food when he could offset it with greasy burgers and fries.

Not to mention the fact that he *loved* burgers and fries. And onion rings, pizza and doughnuts.

Then again, Dani was providing him with the perfect excuse for finishing the run alone.

"What?" Dani didn't hear him. Maybe her ears were clogging up with all those calories she'd stuffed into her mouth last night. Doughnuts wouldn't help, but they'd make her feel better.

She could always run them off later.

"I said to go ahead and call her," he corrected himself smoothly. "I'll just get a few more miles and cool down. See you in an hour or so."

Dani was so relieved she stopped in her tracks. Visions of doughnuts danced in her head as she shouted after Adam, "Don't get lost!" Then, with a definite lift to her spirits, she made a beeline for the doughnut shop.

She was munching happily on her second raised glazed doughnut before even a twinge of guilt surfaced. But it was only a twinge, and she ignored it. After all, it wasn't like she was running around with another man or anything *that* important. She was just concealing a habit from Adam until such time that she felt he wouldn't laugh her out of house and home.

After all, as far as secret vices went, greasy hamburgers, onion rings and doughnuts were fairly mild.

And if he had accepted her explanation for the fracas at the bar last night without question, what could he possibly have to say about a doughnut fetish?

So why was she more nervous now, sneaking off to the local doughnut shop, than she had been last night as she was waiting for him to bail her out of jail?

Nervous but not cowed. Dani limited herself to three of the gooey concoctions. Not out of conscience, but out of financial necessity. That's all she could buy with the dollar bill she had hidden in the toe of her running shoe. The girl at the counter hadn't been all that pleased to accept—much less touch!—the smelly bill, but had backed down under Dani's stare of mean determination.

She was just finishing the last doughnut when she spotted trouble. What was Adam doing coming in here? With her fingers stuffing the last crumbs past her sticky lips, she frantically sorted through the fragments of plots and scenarios that just *might* get her out of this mess. But absolutely nothing came to mind, and she settled for sneaking out the back door.

And it would have worked if Adam hadn't decided to take his own purchase to the back of the store near the rear exit.

"Dani?"

She stopped in her tracks, but didn't turn around. There were still giveaway traces of sugar and crumbs on her lips, and she licked furiously at the evidence.

There was no way out of this. She was well and truly caught, and the only mercy she'd get would be at the discretion of the court. So, in a whirlwind of motion, she turned and threw herself into the arms of one very confused man. There was barely room there, particularly with the paper bag he held clutched to his chest infringing on her space. But whatever was inside was now smashed, and she rested comfortably in Adam's embrace.

Dani didn't pay attention to the smashed bag, more intent upon licking the remaining evidence away from her lips. Maybe she could convince him she'd stopped by for a cup of coffee, she thought, hope raising her spirits a fraction. But the story just wouldn't fly with the sugar bits from her doughnut contradicting her words, and her tongue worked busily until she was sure every last bit of sugar had disappeared. Satisfied it was safe to come up now, Dani gave her lips a last lick and leaned back in his arms. "It worked, didn't it?"

"What worked?" Adam should have expected this. Sneaking in for a doughnut fix was not in the bargain, and now he'd been caught. Or had he? As usual, Adam felt as if he was on the outside looking in, except it appeared he and Dani were the central players and the girl behind the counter their audience.

He wondered how he'd explain the doughnuts he carried, then looked down at the bag he still clutched in one hand—between Dani and his chest. Smashed doughnuts, he amended.

"It worked," she repeated. "I was sitting here over a cup of coffee, wishing you were here, and . . . here you are!" she said brightly, batting her eyes at him to distract his attention from her mouth.

"Coffee?" Dani had stopped for coffee. Adam knew he was sunk now. What would she think of the incriminating doughnuts smashed against her breasts? "I thought you had to call Agnes."

"I remembered she wouldn't be home this late, so I stopped here on my way back." She hoped he wouldn't notice the doughnut shop was on the *other* side of her house from where they had been running.

Coffee. Adam nodded his defeat. He was well and truly caught. Raising his gaze to her face, he was momentarily diverted from his thoughts by the rapid movement of Dani's lashes . . . and a smudge of white on her cheek. White?

"Something in your eye?" he asked casually, not wanting to alert her to his intentions, then leaned forward to touch his tongue to the smudge. Sugar. Dani drank her coffee black, no sugar. Bingo!

"My eye?" she gulped, caught by the powerful arm around her waist as his lips came forward and his tongue tasted her cheek. That was enough to stop the frantic batting of her lashes. This close, all she could concentrate on was the sudden warmth deep inside her, and she waited impatiently for him to move his lips closer to her mouth so she could— Wrong! She stopped herself just in time, jerking back as far as his arm would allow. Essence of doughnut was precisely what Adam would taste if she offered her mouth to him! Close call!

"How did you get sugar on your cheek, love?" he asked huskily, willing her to confess all so he could rescue the doughnuts he'd bought for himself.

"What sugar?" she asked, surprise dripping from her voice. Who me? her expression said, innocent as a newborn babe. Common sense told her the jig was up, but they were playing a game now, and Dani kept to her role.

"On your cheek. I tasted it." She had no intention of coming clean about the doughnut—or doughnuts—he realized. But Adam overcame his disappointment. Watching Dani piece together a story was infinitely more rewarding than true confessions.

"Um, let me see." Dani really didn't expect him to believe her, but this was a contest, with new rules. Besides, Adam looked as though he was enjoying himself. She brightened. It was nice to know she could entertain him so easily. She made the story good. Not believable, just good. "A little boy walked by my table . . . where I was drinking the coffee . . . and stumbled, and his doughnut flew into my face and that's how I got sugar on my cheek." Not bad for impromptu, she congratulated herself, then flashed a challenging smile at Adam. Did he like it, too?

He liked it. "Did he cry?"

"No. I bought him another doughnut." Well, she would have, if it had happened in the first place.

Adam grinned. He was going to love being married to Dani.

"Where'd *you* get the doughnuts?" she asked. She had ignored the bag smashed between them for as long as decently possible. Now it was his turn.

"The counter," he replied instantly, indicating the sales area behind them. It was fun having the upper hand for a change, he thought. "They sell them here."

Dani took a deep breath, not particularly pleased to find herself on the other side of their confusing dialogues. Besides, Adam was stealing all the best lines! "I mean, why do you have doughnuts in that bag? I thought you didn't eat stuff like that."

"I came in for coffee, like you," he said. "And I was the 150th customer of the day."

"So?"

"So every day they give the 150th customer a free bag of doughnuts."

"Uh-huh." Dani nodded. She was beginning to get a feel for the conversation. "And you were going to give them to the first little boy you ran in to?"

"Right."

Simultaneously, they looked around the room. It was empty, that is, if you didn't count the girl behind the counter. Their eyes met, and they laughed.

"No little boys," she said.

"Or little girls," he said.

They grinned.

"And they're smashed now," he warned.

"They probably taste the same," she said innocently.

"Let's find out," he suggested, acting for all the world as if it was a serious experiment.

"I won't tell if you won't," she promised.

"Deal."

11

"SO DID YOU kill anyone you know?"

"Of course not," Dani returned swiftly, indignant that Agnes could think her so careless. But then she remembered that Adam—or Pinhead—had been written into the story long before he had turned up dead. "Well, not really. I had run into him a few times, but we didn't exactly have time for any meaningful conversations." But some people didn't have to talk to communicate, and Dani had felt a strong pull of attraction between them from that first moment at the restaurant.

It was Tuesday, the day "Daniel Carmody" supplied his/her agent with yet another brilliant murder mystery. Dani and Agnes hadn't been seated at their table in the elegant restaurant for more than a few moments before the inquisition started.

A waiter returned with their cocktails, bringing their conversation to a discrete pause. They'd learned from experience that the things they discussed were often misinterpreted, leading to yet another series of embarrassing situations. But it was relatively safe in this restaurant, the waiters and other employees already familiar with their peculiar manner of conversing.

When they were alone, Agnes resumed her interrogation. "I get the impression that you've since found time to . . . get to know each other?"

Dani thoughtfully pushed the ice in her glass around with the blue-and-white striped straw, considering Agnes's question. It was difficult to keep from blurting out the details. Agnes was like family, and Dani had never been able to hide anything important from her family. She swallowed hard, then answered innocently, "Yes, I guess you could say that."

"'Yes, I guess you could say that,'" Agnes mimicked. Leaning forward until her nose was just inches from Dani's face, she threatened. "If you don't tell me, I'll call your mother and tell her you're involved with a man. *That* will get a response!"

"She already knows." Dani grinned a little, amazed at Agnes's threat. She didn't believe it, of course, but it was nice knowing she cared enough to interfere.

"You're kidding!"

"They met over the telephone a few days ago."

"Does she approve?" Agnes asked, knowing she would take her own cue from Dani's mom.

"She didn't say she didn't," she teased, making Agnes work hard for the facts. Dani had taken her mother's silence on the subject as tacit approval—that, and the fact that her brothers hadn't yet arrived on her doorstep.

"This calls for champagne," Agnes stated firmly, signaling the waiter with a flick of her wrist.

Dani wasn't sure the circumstances called for champagne, but then, she wasn't sure they didn't. Likewise, she was reticent about discussing the true extent of her involvement with Adam, mainly because things had changed drastically in the past couple of days. Since Adam had bailed her out of jail, Dani had been less and less aware of her own insecurities.

For the most part, she hadn't even thought about them. The time she spent with Adam was exciting and adventurous and fun, and she didn't want any silly emotional turmoil to spoil it. Instead, she concentrated on enjoying their time together.

"Does he know you killed him?"

"Uh-huh."

"Did he mind?" Agnes had occasionally wondered what kind of man would be able to tolerate Dani's rather unique approach to life. Even as she trusted Dani's judgment, Agnes was dying to meet him. After all, what man in his right mind would fall in love with a woman who had tried to kill him?

"Not really," Dani replied seriously, giving her question the attention it deserved. "At least, I don't think he minded—as long as it wasn't personal," she finished, nodding in confirmation at her own analysis.

Agnes wanted details, and the only ones that didn't make Dani blush were the series of "murders" that led up to Pinhead's demise, not to mention the latest fiasco at the bar. And while it wasn't in Dani's nature to boast of "killings that could have been" or "murders that never happened," she knew Agnes would get a kick out of hearing about them. Editing out the parts that she considered to be private, and therefore irrelevant to the story, Dani embarked upon a recount of her misadventures of the past several weeks. Spurred on by liberal quantities of champagne, Dani waved her arms and made appropriate faces as she told her story. What had seemed frustrating at the time was now an incredibly funny anecdote. And what was even funnier, all that had changed was the telling. The facts remained the same.

Agnes was nearly in hysterics. She particularly liked the part about the blowgun at the theater. "Brilliant, Dani! Absolutely brilliant! Did you write it that way?" she asked, eager to read that particular section of the book.

"Not exactly," Dani confessed. "At the time, I was *not* amused. He was wreaking havoc with my schedule!"

"And what about the bar?" she prodded. The part about getting hauled down to jail hadn't surprised Agnes. She was more amazed that it had taken Dani so long to get arrested. "Did you ever get it right?"

"No, but I've decided to sacrifice a little realism in favor of a dose of prudence," she said seriously. But it had been an easy decision, particularly in view of her time frame. Not to mention Adam's subtle hints about staying out of trouble. "Adam promised the cops I wouldn't do anything stupid, at least not before they decide what to do about the charges."

"They'll drop them in the end," Agnes volunteered. "They always do."

"Yeah," Dani agreed, grinning at the new charges that decorated her police record. Inciting to riot was the least of her worries. It was a trumped-up charge in the first place, primarily because it had been more a matter of the bar patrons taking sides than a full-scale riot. And since they'd all taken Dani's side, the only person getting picked on was Big and Brawny.

The assault charge had already been dropped, mainly because the police were incapable of swallowing the idea of Dani attacking Big and Brawny.

Agnes giggled again, then poured some more champagne. "You've never told me what Adam had to say about this. Did he get curious about the charges on your rap sheet?"

Dani had the grace to blush before she buried her face behind the tall menu the maître d' had left on the table. Agnes always did manage to hit on subjects Dani would have preferred to avoid.

She put the menu back on the white linen tablecloth. "I, er, I haven't exactly discussed it with him," she said hesitantly.

"Haven't discussed it with him?" Agnes didn't believe this one. "How could he not be curious about your colorful history as recorded by the Denver Police Department?"

"Well, he didn't actually see my record," Dani explained, not about to confess to the fancy footwork that had prevented Adam from knowing anything more than the most recent charges.

"You *lied* to him?" Agnes was aghast at Dani's evasion. Firm foundations were not built on omissions and deceit.

"Not really," she hurriedly defended herself. "I just thought there might be a better time for true confessions," she finished weakly. Like never, she wished silently, uncomfortably aware that her hopes in that direction were doomed.

Agnes satisfied herself with an inelegant harumph, letting Dani know what she thought about her response. "So when do I get to meet Adam...Adam what?"

"Adam. Adam Winters. And I promise you'll meet him soon. In fact," she added, a regretful note creeping into her voice, "he was going to join us for lunch today, but something came up at the office at the last minute." Adam had practically run out of the house, giving her no more idea what the pressing business was than he had before. It grated on Dani, and she was determined to bring it into the open when she saw him again.

"Well, you can't hold a man's job against him," Agnes pronounced.

Dani brightened considerably at the sight of food, and dove into the steaming plate of cannelloni with complete disregard for Agnes's moan of envy. Her friend was perpetually on a diet, and Dani was convinced she arranged these luncheon meetings just to remind herself of what she was missing!

Gossiping with Agnes was one of her favorite pastimes, and Dani pretty much forgot to eat as she found herself laughing hysterically at the tidbits of information Agnes managed to accumulate. Not only did Agnes possess a gold mine of stories about the publishing industry, but her ribald comments about prominent happenings in Denver society were mostly beyond belief— not because they weren't true, but because they were! And by the time Dani completed her own slightly embellished version of the encounter with Big and Brawny, the two women were giggling helplessly.

After one too many noisy outbursts of uncontrollable laughter, Dani and Agnes subsided into the occasional giggle as they dutifully drank the complimentary coffee the maître d' had sent to their table. This gentle hint of reproof had brought its own share of unladylike guffaws before they finally settled down and drank the restorative brew.

It was a much more subdued Dani who said goodbye to Agnes just a few minutes later. The combination of alcohol in the middle of the day and the unaccustomed series of nights she had spent in Adam's arms—doing nearly everything *but* sleep—had finally taken its toll. Giving her agent first dibs on the cab that was parked outside the door, Dani returned to the restaurant's ladies' room to await her own taxi.

If Dani had remained outside the canopy she might never have seen the couple in the restaurant's lounge. She spotted them the second she emerged from the ladies' room into the softly lit hallway. An angled view of the bar area made them invisible to the people that walked in the front door, but Dani was coming from the opposite direction.

She had no problem seeing them. None at all.

Perhaps if he had been sitting with his back to her, she just might have missed him. And as tired as she was, Dani probably wouldn't have paused for a better look even if the back of his head had struck a note of familiarity. It would have been a puzzle to amuse her on the ride home, nothing more.

In profile, Adam was immediately recognizable.

But Dani didn't have a clue who the woman was. In fact, about all she noticed in that first split second was the delicate, ring-laden hand that was resting possessively on Adam's forearm. It was the intimacy of this gesture that stopped Dani from charging forward to tell him she was there.

He had said he was working, Dani remembered. Working. But the scene in front of her eyes didn't resemble her idea of work.

Stepping back into the shadows of the hall, she expelled the breath she'd been holding, fighting to control the wave of misery that surged within her heart. She didn't worry about being seen. They were too engrossed in each other to notice anyone else, particularly someone who was standing still as a statue in the dimly lit hallway.

Vague impressions of silky black hair framing an incredibly beautiful face flitted through Dani's head, but she was too absorbed in staring at Adam to pay the woman much more attention. He was bent slightly forward, as if listening intently to what she was telling him. The eyes, the curve of his mouth, the slightly slanting brow were all as she remembered—then again, they were different. Dani noticed the arm he'd rested on the table slowly withdrawing as his hand carried a drink to his lips. Long slender fingers tipped with vermillion nails were left to fondle the polished table top when his arm didn't return to its former resting place.

Dani switched her attention to the woman, surprised at the brief grimace of impatience that was hidden from Adam as he turned to summon the waiter.

"Miss, your cab is waiting."

Dani only half heard the summons. Her thoughts were in the next room, confusing swirls of questions without answers.

"Miss..." The doorman raised his voice, and Dani suddenly realized she was in danger of being seen. And, of course, that wouldn't do at all. She had an aversion to airing her private humiliation in public places.

FIVE CUPS OF COFFEE, a cold shower and a miserable run through the park were all part of the coordinated effort Dani made to wash the effects of alcohol from her system. Her first temptation had been to open the bottle of twelve-year-old Scotch she'd been saving, but somehow drinking herself into a stupor didn't have any appeal. Besides, she usually fell asleep if she overdrank her limit, and the champagne had come perilously close to accomplishing that already.

Besides, Dani didn't want to sleep. She wanted to think . . . well, she really didn't *want* to think, but reasoned it was probably the mature way to handle the situation. Even when she had found Greg in the arms of that gorgeous cheerleader, Dani had managed to maintain her dignity. She was nearly seven years older now, and there was no way she could justify handling this situation any differently.

So she drank coffee, suffered through the cold shower and ran. Finally, after another shower, warm this time, she was left with nothing to do but think—something she had avoided by focusing her energies on diluting the champagne in her system. Carrying yet another cup of coffee into the living room, she sat down on the sofa and curled her legs beneath her.

The place that had given her so much pleasure, both in its creation and its welcoming familiarity, might just as well have been a stranger's home for all the comfort it yielded. And Dani would never again be able to look at her home without remembering Adam. She didn't think that would make life very easy.

An ivory tower, he'd once called it. It felt more like a prison.

She had no one to blame but herself, she knew. From that very first meeting, she had freely opened herself to his companionship, to his presence. That first afternoon he'd arrived on her doorstep she could have shut the door. Or, if she'd simply stalled his advances by leaving him downstairs in the "waiting" room, this wouldn't have happened.

But her common sense had flown out the window the first time he'd touched her, and only now was it returning ... on a tidal wave of self-recrimination.

She had lost control. She had begun to trust Adam without even realizing she was doing it. All her resolutions about control and restraint had been nothing more than empty words.

Attraction, love, trust—the triangle was complete. It didn't take a fool to figure that out. Why else was she hurting so badly?

She couldn't even pretend what she felt was anger. Not anymore. She was hurt because she had been betrayed. Again.

It occurred to her that at least the men in her life turned to incredibly beautiful women when they left her. She didn't know whether to be flattered by their implied standards, or resentful that she apparently hadn't measured up.

She wondered when Adam was coming home, and what she would say when he did. Could she ignore what she'd seen in the restaurant, pretend it hadn't happened?

No. Even if she could hide the truth from herself, she would never be able to hide it from Adam. A shattered heart wasn't that easy to conceal.

Would she quietly tell Adam what she'd witnessed in the restaurant, then leave him to pack his few belongings, forcing him to accept without recourse an abrupt end to their relationship? Would Adam see the accusation in her eyes and leave without protest? Or would he argue with her, try to justify his actions?

He'd told her he had to work. How could he argue his way out of that one? The quickening beat of her heart alerted her to an angle she hadn't yet considered. What if he *had* been working?

With startling clarity, it came to her. Things were no longer confused. The link between past and present was finally severed as Dani recognized one very important fact. She loved Adam, and all that nonsense about being able to love without trusting was precisely that: nonsense! One didn't work without the other. One was as necessary as the other.

She loved him, and more important at the moment, she *trusted* him.

A flash of panic tore through her as Dani realized that so far, the trust appeared to be one-sided. Adam had never said anything about being in love with her. But that didn't necessarily mean he didn't love her. Perhaps he had been waiting for her to make the first move, or maybe he was waiting to make sure of his own feelings. Either way, Dani didn't allow herself to worry. Hadn't he showed her in a thousand ways that he loved her? Nonverbal communication. Adam was an expert at it.

As for all that rot about him not trusting her enough to share his professional life, Dani was beginning to think he hadn't thought about it beyond keeping the confidential information confidential.

Feeling like a boob, she grinned with anticipation at the prospect of Adam's homecoming. They had so much to talk about, she couldn't even begin to decide where to start. She wanted to tell him about her rap sheet, confess the fast-food fetish was not limited to doughnuts, admit her fears about his job. They were all important issues, and she was in a tizzy of excitement at the thought of getting all that off her chest. She glanced at her watch and her heart sank with the realization that Adam wasn't due home until much later that evening. Because he had a dinner meeting.

Taking a deep breath, Dani cautiously approached the subject. It wouldn't do to let her suspicions ruin a perfectly good confession of love, and Dani was determined to deal with them. Starting with what she had seen that afternoon. Adam had been working, so who was the woman? Could she have been a client?

No. She rejected that idea, giving Adam credit for a more businesslike approach to his job. He just didn't seem the type to play games while conducting a business lunch. Did Dani know so much about his sense of honor? Yes, she decided, she did know that much about Adam. He would never compromise his professional integrity by involving himself with a client.

Perhaps she'd been an old friend, a former lover. But no, Adam had told her it was business.

Was she a secretary? One of his investigators? Neither of those possibilities rang true. Once again, Dani knew without a single doubt that Adam wouldn't involve himself in an intimate relationship with an employee. Not only was it bad business sense, but the inevitable complications were unwelcome in any office.

So what was she left with if she ruled out employee, client, friend or lover? What was she missing?

The criminally inclined portion of Dani's mind finally hit upon what should have been the obvious solution. Adam had either been meeting with an informer, or was actually investigating the woman herself!

The day outside noticeably brightened in the moment of her enlightenment, lending Mother Nature's glowing approval to her deductions. The wasted hours she'd spent in an emotional slump were miraculously forgotten in the joy of discovery. Adam hadn't been lying to her. And he *wasn't* seeing another woman, not in the sense she'd assumed.

They still had a chance for a life together!

Then Dani sobered as she realized that she was still faced with the possibility that Adam didn't love her in return.

Or, just maybe, he didn't love her *yet*. Well, there was certainly something she could do about that! Resolved to make her own feelings clear to him the first chance she had, Dani dashed into the bedroom and began ransacking her closet in hopes of finding something casually sexy to wear. It was sheer luck that the telephone rang before she'd made a complete shambles of her closet.

"I'm sorry, love."

It didn't matter what he said. Dani was just thankful to hear his voice, to hear the sensual caress that resounded in the endearment. Dani choked back a sob of relief that he'd called, totally unable to respond, not having the faintest idea why he was sorry. It wasn't important. She loved him.

"Dani, are you there?" His voice now carried a slightly worried edge, and she brushed aside her melodramatic mood.

"Of course," she said, then ad-libbed an excuse for her silence. "I was just napping." He'd buy that, Dani reckoned, since she'd set quite an astonishing pattern for napping at all hours of the day. But she couldn't stop herself from asking, "Why are you sorry?" She wasn't worried, but a little curiosity was always healthy.

"Because I'm here at the office and you're home alone," he said, sounding perfectly wretched at the notion. "I thought I'd get done early enough to spend some time with you, but things kind of got complicated around here. I'll just have enough time to change here at the office before going back out tonight."

Dani was suddenly aware of an astonishingly powerful wave of jealousy lapping at her soul. Cold, identifiable jealousy. She didn't bother to deny it to herself, but managed to keep this new awareness from influencing the tone of her voice.

"Is it the same case that's kept you busy all day?" she asked. No sense wasting a jealous rage if it was a perfectly boring dinner meeting with a seventy-three-year-old *male* client!

"Yes," he breathed heavily in what Dani immediately recognized as a combination of exhaustion and frustration. "But tonight should really be the last meeting," he said hopefully. "I can't stand much more of this case. It's driving me crazy."

It was the most he'd ever said about the investigation, and Dani sincerely believed his desire to be finished with it. But that didn't make her feel any better. They talked wistfully for a few moments more, then hung up.

Dani sat gingerly on the bed and reviewed her most recent discovery. She was jealous, terribly so, of the woman with whom Adam would spend the evening. It wasn't a matter of not trusting Adam—she'd already run that obstacle course and was satisfied with the results. But that black-haired witch with the brightly painted claws didn't appear the least bit trustworthy.

Unfortunately there was nothing Dani could do about it. Just as she'd dealt with the emotions of love and trust, she was determined to eradicate the jealous green monster from her thoughts.

She rose from her perch on the bed and moved back toward the closet, intent upon restoring some order to the mangled clothes. Replacing the items she'd pulled out just moments earlier, she lectured herself severely. Jealousy was *not* an acceptable emotion. It was childish. It was immature.

It was real.

The more Dani thought about it, the more she realized it wouldn't go away just by wishing. And her willpower was very nearly exhausted for the day.

The solution came to her so forcefully that it rocked her back on her heels and nearly laid her flat with its power. There *was* something she could do about it.

She could kill her.

12

DANI MADE A MINUTE ADJUSTMENT to the brown wig, peering into the rearview mirror to make a final check for telltale wisps of blond hair. No, everything was in place. Pushing the mirror back into position, she slipped out of the car and walked quickly across the parking lot toward the restaurant.

She hadn't bothered with an elaborate costume. There was no need. There had been no time to case the restaurant, no script to write, no preliminary groundwork to perform. Armed with a plan that had already failed twice, Dani marched bravely toward her confrontation with the fates.

The only real danger would lie in Adam's recognizing her, but Dani was confident that the wig would give her the protection she needed. After all, he'd be too busy with whatever plan he had up his own sleeve to give any attention to an unknown brunette seated at the bar.

Dani knew where Adam was dining that night. He had mentioned both the restaurant name and time on the telephone earlier that day. That information was priceless now, particularly in view of her intentions.

At first the inspired notion of killing the woman had been too ludicrous to give serious thought. Dani had summarily dismissed the idea and was even a bit ashamed at herself for thinking of it in the first place. For nearly two minutes she had ridiculed the notion, calling it immature, petty and idiotic.

But in the end, the idea appealed to her sense of justice. The idea of "murdering" someone against whom she had a grievance was entirely new to Dani. She'd always been removed from her victims, preferring to deal with murder in the abstract rather than as an intimate act of vengeance. Her murderers had been professionals, accustomed to delivering one body, perhaps more, but always for a price.

If she succeeded, it could form the basis for a new type of villain. Her readers would be completely fooled, because they'd be looking for a passionless murderer, not someone with a personal motive.

If she succeeded, her own feelings of satisfaction would outdistance any misgivings. True, it was immature, petty and idiotic. But it wouldn't actually harm anyone and, with a bit of luck, the victim wouldn't even know she'd been killed.

But Dani would know. And that's all that mattered. All the same, she crossed her fingers that Adam wouldn't kill *her* if things went wrong.

Shifting aside any second thoughts, Dani pushed open the door to the restaurant and found herself in a brightly lit foyer. To her left was the entrance to the dining room, but it was the lounge opposite that drew her. Adam had arranged to take the woman there for cocktails, and Dani stepped cautiously across the doorway.

It was a large room, identical to hundreds of bars across the country, complete with tiny tables and leather swivel chairs. Masses of small trees and hanging plants alluded to a sense of privacy that was at the same time contradicted by the sheer size of the room. A gleaming grand piano stood in one corner, and Dani was surprised to see a distinguished gentleman seated at the ivory keys softly generating the familiar notes of a theme song to a current popular romantic movie. It seemed too early, too quiet for the evening's entertainment to begin.

But then, it all depended upon what one considered to be entertainment. Dani had her own ideas on that subject and blocked the sweetly romantic melody out of her mind. A theme song from some Hitchcock thriller would have been more appropriate.

Swiftly taking inventory of the customers, she smothered a brief flare of panic and made her way toward the bar opposite the piano, casually perusing its length. The seats were nearly empty. More important, the seat Dani needed was not taken.

Adam wasn't there yet. But then, she hadn't expected him to be. The lack of preplanning had forced her to arrive early in order to stake out a decent vantage point as well as to calculate the sequence of events.

The murder was modeled on the poisoning she'd attempted before. Given the opportunity, Dani would empty the vial into what she deduced was the woman's drink. She trusted she was familiar enough with Adam's tastes to discern which beverage would be his.

It was simply a matter of luck and timing. She hopped onto the bar stool, reflecting briefly on her battle with Big and Brawny. That was one complication she was glad to do without, Dani thought as she smiled politely at the bartender. The cocktail service station was on her right. The plan was beginning to look feasible.

She had worn a dress Adam had never seen. It hadn't been difficult to select one—he'd only seen her in the green silk and the black. For tonight, she'd chosen another silk dress, sapphire blue this time. The color did strange things to her eyes, lending a violet accent to the green irises. It was startling, but Dani didn't give it any thought. If he bothered to look, Adam would be deceived by the brown hair. In any case, she didn't intend to get that close. This was simply a case of murder and exit, fast and clean.

Taking small sips of wine from the glass the bartender had supplied, Dani turned in her seat so she could watch the door out of the corner of her eye. There were few customers in the lounge, some of them obviously waiting for companions and dates, others paired or in small groups of three and four. She figured the numbers would increase dramatically when the after-dinner crowd drifted across the hall to listen to the piano. As she watched, the maître d' from the restaurant came in to escort a party of four to their table in the dining room.

"I'll buy you a drink if you'll just let me look into your eyes for the next hour or so."

Dani was so startled she nearly fell off the stool, but caught herself in time to avoid that embarrassment. Turning her head, she found the source of the voice. It was one of the men she had noticed earlier. Either he'd given up on his date, or he hadn't been waiting for one after all. Of medium height with sandy-blond hair, he was one of the more handsome men she'd seen in recent years. But she wasn't even interested enough to give him a one-to-ten rating. Not tonight. Not ever.

She favored him with a brilliant but kindly smile, then said, "Sorry. I'm meeting someone."

That didn't stop him. Of course Dani should have realized that anyone with such a corny pickup line wouldn't be deterred with a simple "no."

"So I'll keep you company until he comes."

Dani threw tact and subtlety to the wind. She didn't have time to fool around with trying to get rid of this masher in a polite fashion. "Get lost," she said with a smile—this one cool to the point of freezing—then turned her back to him. She didn't bother to check to see if he'd taken her gentle hint. She was too busy watching the couple entering the lounge.

Adam was positively elegant in his dark suit and brilliant white shirt. Even the discretely striped tie was a welcome sight to Dani, knowing that it would be her own fingers that loosened the knot later that night. A warm wave of sensual awareness rolled through her, diverting her thoughts to a room a few miles away, to a bed that was waiting to welcome the lovers home.

But first things first. She had a job to do. Tearing her eyes away from Adam, she carefully studied her victim. Tightly wrapped in a bright red dress—well, *partly* wrapped—she strolled at Adam's side, hanging onto his arm with an eagerness that Dani found hard to stomach. They moved together toward the piano where Adam helped the woman slide into one of the leather chairs. Taking the other for himself, he let his eyes drift around the room.

Although Adam was not presently looking in her direction, Dani took no chances and twisted to face the bar. Out of the corner of her eye, she saw the cocktail waitress approach their table. There wasn't much time now, and her fingers sought the small vial inside her purse. The waitress was quick. Dani palmed the vial just as she returned to the work station.

"Kirin and a martini, up." And just as soon as she'd spoken, the waitress was gone, moving easily toward a newly arrived trio that had taken a table in the far corner.

A slow smile spread across Dani's face, soon becoming a radiant flash of sheer pleasure. She took a second to thank the fates for their guidance, and patiently waited for the drink order to be filled.

"BEER?" Stephanie said on a note of disbelief. "Before dinner?" As much as she tried to hide it, her disapproval rang out clearly. What she was really saying was "Only yokels and slobs drink beer before a gourmet dinner."

Adam didn't much care what she thought. It was no longer important to impress her. It was the last night he'd have to spend with her. Even if their plan failed, he wouldn't have to continue in his role of millionaire playboy.

Tonight, they would force Holbrook and Channing into a surprise confrontation. Waiting for them to make contact had brought them no results, and Baxter had approved this last-ditch effort.

No, Adam didn't care what Stephanie thought. Besides, the beer reminded him of Dani, and that helped make the time away from her more bearable.

Shrugging off her comment with the ease of a man comfortable with himself and his tastes, he swiveled slightly in his chair to check out the room. There was only a scattering of customers at this hour. In fact, Adam could count exactly eight "real" customers. In addition to those, he identified a half dozen of his own people— four of them paired into couples and two men sitting at either end of the bar. One of the pairs was seated at a table near enough to his that eavesdropping was not only possible, it was practically unavoidable. The other couple had maneuvered themselves into a position that was reasonably close to the sandy-haired man sitting alone at the bar.

The man was Sam Holbrook. The bag man. The accomplice.

Stephanie was chattering again, and Adam forced himself to pick up the threads of her conversation. It wouldn't do to blow the whole plan by upsetting her now. But it didn't take all of his concentration to murmur an occasional comment or nod in agreement, and he let his eyes slip away from the black mane of hair that she had pulled tightly away from her face, a dark imitation of Eva Peron's famous trademark. It suited her, Adam had to admit. But then, he had never disputed the fact that she was a beautiful woman.

That didn't make her desirable to him. For that matter, it didn't even make her interesting.

Not like the woman seated at the bar. There was something about her that drew Adam's stare. The silky mass of brown hair wasn't familiar, nor could he recall ever having seen the sapphire dress. But the slender length of her legs, the gentle curve of her bottom.... Just two weeks ago, he'd seen legs like that for the first time in his life, and now he was seeing an identical pair. He wanted to go over to the woman and put his arms around her, pull her back into his hard warmth, let her know the extent of his sudden arousal.

He swore under his breath, wishing violently that she'd face him so he could dispel the illusion that it was Dani sitting there and dampen the fires of his desire to a more comfortable level.

Adam shook his head in mild self-reproof before turning back to Stephanie. It must be the tension that made him see something of Dani in a total stranger.

But that "something" was exciting. Desirable and sensuous. He couldn't wait until the evening was over and he could race home to Dani and tell her about his fantasy.

Later.

It was nearly time to get this show on the road. Adam's men had managed to learn about Holbrook's plan with little trouble. The tap on his hotel telephone had taken care of that problem. Having Holbrook in Denver was a bonus they hadn't anticipated, and with time running out, it was the perfect place to stage a confrontation between the blackmailing partners.

The bad news was Holbrook's purpose for visiting this bar. From what they had been able to decipher from his telephone conversations, it was apparent that he was peddling something, probably pills or powders, and the people he supplied were to meet him here.

That discovery made it imperative they finish their own operation at the first opportunity. If the police picked him up before they connected him with the Channing woman, they'd lose their chance. And the police were interested in him. Adam's men had stumbled across their trail more than once over the past week.

That was okay. If all went as planned tonight, the police could have him.

Adam's plan was simple. He'd leave the room to make a phone call. He calculated neither Channing nor Holbrook would pass up that opportunity for a quick conference. After all, they'd been avoiding each other for weeks, and the coincidence of both of them showing up at the same restaurant would be bound to shake them up. They weren't professionals, and wouldn't react as such. A professional wouldn't take the bait whereas an amateur wouldn't recognize it for what it was. His people were strategically placed for eavesdropping. He could only hope that his calculations were correct.

He knew he was right. He had sensed the brief stiffening in the woman at his side when they'd entered the room and she'd recognized her accomplice. It hadn't been as easy to judge Holbrook's reactions from that distance. But a quick double take followed by his studied indifference to their entrance had been the giveaway. Stephanie Channing was simply too beautiful for any of the men present to totally ignore her. And not a man there would take his eyes off the outrageous display of white skin she flaunted. The daringly tight dress she wore attracted the eyes of every man in the lounge—that is, all but one. By totally ignoring her, Holbrook proved rather than denied their association. It was a stupid mistake, one that only an amateur would have made.

The cocktail waitress was returning with their drinks, and Adam roused himself to interrupt Stephanie's long-running commentary on the diamond bracelet she'd seen that afternoon while shopping. Too bad, he mused. She really thought he'd buy it for her. Greedy woman. It was time for her downfall.

"What the hell did you put in that drink?"

The accusation was loud and disbelieving. Looking past the cocktail waitress who was just reaching their table, Adam sought the source of the disturbance with a sinking sensation of incredulity in the pit of his stomach.

It was déjà vu in nightmare proportions.

As Adam watched, the waitress paused to observe the commotion back at the bar. For that matter, everyone in the lounge, including one horrified Stephanie, watched as Sam Holbrook pulled the protesting woman in the blue dress off the bar stool and down the aisle toward their table.

Unruly masses of brown hair obscured her face, but Adam didn't need to see it. He knew if he looked hard enough, if he pulled away that ridiculous wig, green eyes would capture his and brilliantly flash their defiant message.

Adam closed his eyes, silently praying that when he opened them again, everything would be back to normal. That what was happening was simply another fantasy his mind had woven around the woman at the bar in the sapphire blue dress. That Dani wasn't being dragged across the lounge to confront her latest victim.

That she wasn't ruining their last chance of proving the Channing woman was the blackmailer.

He opened his eyes, and silently admitted defeat. Dani was standing there, her wrist in the firm possession of Sam Holbrook. And by the way she was studiously avoiding his eyes, Adam knew without a doubt that this was no random murder attempt. He didn't stop to question how she had gotten wind of the information that enable her to be here at this critical moment. Dani was a talented and imaginative woman, and he couldn't hold that against her. But he did wonder why she had taken the trouble to reenact her poisoning routine. No matter, he'd get the truth out of her later.

A quick glance showed Stephanie had recovered none of her composure. All in all, everything was perfectly poised for disaster.

"She poisoned your drink!"

Adam sighed. This wasn't going to get any better. Dani's technique could definitely stand some improvement. Maybe he could work with her on that. If he didn't kill her first. The eerie silence that had greeted Holbrook's accusation extended to include the woman shackled at his side, and Adam could only pray she'd stay that way. He tried to signal a warning with his eyes, but her attention was definitely focused on other things.

"Sam, if this is some kind of a joke. . . ."

Stephanie had recovered now, and her words knocked Adam sideways. Sam. She'd said Sam. But that was just proof of acquaintance. He needed more.

He didn't have long to wait.

"It's no joke, Stephanie!"

Where had she heard that name before? Dani wondered.

The hand that held Dani's jerked her forward, and Adam resisted the urge to leap out of his chair and break his nose. But things were moving fast, and he satisfied himself with merely postponing his impulse. Holbrook wouldn't hurt her in front of witnesses. "I saw her put something in your drink!"

"I didn't . . ." Dani meekly retreated back into silence when she felt the full weight of three disbelieving stares. She might as well face it. This was a no-win situation. The masher had caught her, much in the same fashion as Adam had caught her before. The cocktail waitress hadn't even managed to deliver the drink. She appeared to have been struck by the same paralysis that affected nearly everyone else in the bar.

Not that it mattered. It appeared the masher knew Scarlet Claws—Dani's personalized nickname for the witch with Adam—and he hadn't let her drink it anyway.

She didn't even dare look at Adam. He'd probably murder her for this stunt.

Dani figured this probably wasn't the most opportune moment to tell Adam she loved him. Maybe later, after he killed her.

"Don't be stupid, Sam." The woman was ignoring both Adam and Dani, her almond-shaped cat's eyes narrowing on the masher.

Dani could almost hear the wheels clicking in the woman's head, but she didn't have a clue what was going on in there. A surreptitious peek at Adam made her keep her mouth shut. To her utter amazement, the beginnings of a smile were beginning to form on his face as he watched the woman at his side with absolute concentration.

It wasn't hard to guess that Adam knew something that Dani didn't. She wondered what he was waiting for.

"I'm *not* being stupid!" the masher insisted. "I *saw* her put something in your drink!"

The barmaid looked suspiciously at the drink in question, skillfully turning the tray so that it was on the other side, just in case.

"Who'd want to poison me?" Scarlet Claws scoffed, the ridicule heavy in her voice.

Me, you silly woman, Dani said silently. It occurred to her that she felt better than she'd felt all day. Maybe jealousy wasn't a healthy emotion, but revenge was terrific. Even if it hadn't worked, it was the thought that counted.

She let her arm go limp, hoping the weight would tire him out. Dani was willing to try anything to get his slimy fingers off her skin, and scratching his eyes out in public wasn't a very ladylike gesture. Instead of freeing her, he just gripped her wrist tighter.

"Baxter!" he shouted. "It's got to be!"

"Shut up, you idiot!" The woman hissed furiously at the masher, and Dani was privately relieved Scarlet Claws's eyes weren't focused on her. They were deadly! Anyway, who was Baxter?

The man didn't take her advice and expanded on his theory. "The old man figured it out and decided it was cheaper to get rid of you than to pay you off," he explained, confidence growing with every word. "Don't you see, Steff?"

But she wasn't paying attention to him anymore. Those deadly eyes had found another mark. Dani decided the masher was as harmless as a flea compared to his friend.

"*Did* Baxter send you?" Her words were softer now, but no less lethal. But she didn't wait for an answer. "Because if he did, it's going to cost him a whole lot more than the first time," she snarled, daring Dani to deny the accusation.

"Who's Baxter?" Dani asked on cue.

"I think that's enough," Adam said quietly, then stood and approached Dani and the masher. "Take your hands off her, Holbrook."

The man didn't comply. Dani wasn't even certain he was listening. For that matter, Dani herself was having trouble following the script. "How do you know my name?" was the man's only reply to Adam's demand.

Adam didn't answer, but simply stood his ground, repeating his request. "I said, get your hands off the lady.

Now." Not even the masher could escape the implied threat of his words.

Dani was released a split second later, but was destined to be disappointed if she thought Adam would pay her any attention. Instead, he turned away and spoke with the couple at the next table.

"Did you get all of that?" he asked.

"You bet, boss," the woman replied, pulling a cassette recorder out of her handbag. "Every word."

Adam nodded his satisfaction, inordinately pleased that his relief was hidden behind a professional facade. It had been touch and go there for a while, but there was no need to let everyone know just how out of control the situation had been.

"The police will be here shortly, Adam." Chuck had joined the party at the table, and the other men made a loose circle around them. Chuck hesitated for a moment, then asked, "What do I tell them about the, um, poisoning?"

"She's mine," Adam said quietly. "My problem. I'll take care of her."

When Chuck opened his mouth to argue, Adam further defined the situation. "That," he sighed, "is Dani."

Of course, that put an entirely different light on the subject. Chuck stared.

Adam spared a glance at Stephanie Channing, and was rewarded with a malevolent glare. That was okay. She was keeping her mouth shut now, and he couldn't be more pleased. Luckily for Adam, she hadn't had the same sense earlier.

There was a slight scuffle as Sam Holbrook finally realized the depth of his predicament, but Adam's men were there to keep him from making too big of a ruckus.

Everything was under control. He could let Chuck take over now. The police would soon arrive, and Adam's men would hand over the culprits and the evidence of blackmail at the same time. He could call Baxter in California the next morning with the news—if the police didn't beat him to it. Adam had a few words with Chuck, then turned to find Dani hovering around the edge of the circle. "Let's go, Danielle."

"I haven't finished my drink." As far as delaying tactics went, it was weak. But Dani was desperate for any excuse right now that would keep them under the watchful eyes of responsible citizens. She was pretty sure Adam wouldn't kill her in public.

"Fine." A drink sounded good to Adam, too. He'd been looking forward to that Kirin. Taking Dani by the elbow, he started to escort her back to her place at the bar. A few steps, then he paused. "Take it off."

"What?" she squealed, not having a clue what he was talking about.

"The hair. Take it off." His fingers tightened around her elbow, and Dani knew he intended to have his way. Sparing an embarrassed glance at the curious onlookers, Dani dug her fingers into the thick strands of her scalp and pulled. Blond hair fell in heavy waves to her shoulders, cascading down her back as it was loosened from its confinement. Dani tossed the wig onto the table in front of the black-haired woman, then turned back to Adam before she could gauge her reaction.

Without a word, he thrust his fingers into the golden waves, roughly combing them into a semblance of order. Briefly, he let his fingers warm her scalp. Now everything was in order. Instead of a woman who resembled Dani in certain features, he had the real thing.

It also didn't hurt to expose her real appearance to the men and women that worked for him. Who knew what the future would hold, and the sooner they learned to recognize Dani, the safer everyone would be.

"What about this drink?" The cocktail waitress was still standing there with the questionable beverage on her tray. Adam's lips crooked into a smile as he lifted the glass from the tray and turned to Dani.

"I hate martinis," she said clearly, correctly interpreting his intentions.

"Tough," he growled, then stepped closer and guided the glass to her mouth. There was an audible gasp from the spellbound crowd as Dani's lips touched the rim. "Drink it," he ordered, smothering his amusement at her heightened color.

She had no choice. Dani sipped, then gulped as the angle of the glass was abruptly raised. Half the drink was gone before he lowered the glass. Neither of them were aware of the general sigh of relief that Dani was still standing, but there was a tense expectancy in the air—as if they were just waiting for her to keel over.

Dani took pride in the fact that she managed to keep from choking. It wasn't easy. The watered-down martini was worse than she had expected, but nothing on earth would make her admit it to Adam. And she had no intention of letting him think he was getting away with anything. "That's three."

Adam winced at the revival of the mule story. But the heated promise in her eyes was enough to make him look forward to his punishment.

"Still want that drink?" he asked as he returned the unfinished martini to the waitress.

"Not really."

"Let's go." Without another word, he reclaimed her elbow and steered her firmly toward the door and out of the restaurant. If his memory served him, they had Kirin at home. All in all, it was probably a better place to hold the lecture and/or argument he was planning. Then they wouldn't have to drive anywhere before they made up.

His car was parked in the street out front, and Dani knew better than to suggest she reclaim her own. For that matter, she decided that keeping her mouth shut was her best strategy for the time being.

"We'll talk at home." As if she needed encouragement to keep quiet! But he'd said home, not "at the house," not "at your place." Home.

He used his own key to let them in the front door, and they mounted the steps together. Dani wondered what he'd do if she just turned and put her arms around him. But the forbidding look on his face as he turned to confront her prevented Dani from putting her thoughts into action.

"I want you to repeat after me," he said, firmly grasping her shoulders. "I will never again interfere in an investigation." That was the first step. He waited for her to take it.

"I love you." There, she'd said it. Dani stared into Adam's eyes with a hint of challenge. Now it was his turn.

Adam blinked once, then again. Those weren't the precise words he had expected to hear. "That's nice, Dani. But we'll talk about that later," he said patiently, controlling his own instincts to pull her into his hard warmth. He curbed his own desires because he had to get his point across to Dani. Things might have gotten out of hand. It might have been a dangerous investigation instead of simply a touchy one. And Dani might have gotten hurt. "Now repeat after me—I will never again interfere with an investigation."

Dani sighed, wishing he'd get out of lecture mode and into a more romantic mood. After all, she had just told him she loved him. Didn't he care?

"Dani?" He was still waiting, but his patience was wearing thin. There were so many other things he'd rather be doing now, but this was important.

"Oh, all right!" she huffed. Did he *always* have to do things his way? "I won't ever interfere in an investigation." Then she repeated her earlier words, just in case he'd missed them the first time. "I love you, Adam." And leaning forward, she closed the distance between them, working her arms up around his neck until her hands were clasped.

"Are you saying that so I won't yell at you for nearly ruining things tonight?" Her timing *was* a bit suspicious.

"Of course not." She smiled against his chin, and Adam suddenly felt the nip of sharp teeth in the same place. "I just thought now was a good time to tell you. I wanted to say something earlier, but Scarlet Claws was in the way."

Scarlet Claws? Adam was puzzled, then amused. Dani had a gift for hanging tags on people. He wondered what she called him behind his back.

Reaching up, he unclasped her hands and pulled her arms away. "We have to talk."

Dani consulted her watch. "Five minutes." That's about how long she could wait to hear Adam say the words she needed to hear.

Five minutes. Adam considered her limit seriously, then nodded his head in agreement. He could wait that long before claiming her lips, tasting her mouth. Maybe.

Leading the way to the sofa, he shucked his jacket and pulled Dani down beside him onto the soft cushions. Five minutes. At least the drapes were already closed.

Before he could ask, Dani blurted out her version of the story. "I saw you at lunch and was jealous, but you said you were working so I figured she was part of the job, but that didn't make it better because she looked like she wanted to eat you and that made me mad, so I decided to get even."

Adam stared open-mouthed at Dani, amazed that she could get the whole thing out without stopping for a single breath. It made sense. At least, taking Dani's undoubtedly warped viewpoint, it all fit. But that didn't mean it was right.

"You could have ruined everything." He tried to inject a note of reprimand into his voice, but his thoughts were already on her confession and what he was going to say to her when the five minutes were up.

Dani still wasn't sure what everything was, but that didn't stop her from pointing out the obvious. "But I didn't, did I."

"No, Dani, you didn't," he admitted. In fact, the stuff they'd gotten on tape was enough to convict both of them. But he wasn't going to let her off so easy. "That still doesn't make it right."

"It wouldn't have happened at all if you had given me a hint about what you were doing. I spent the last week worried sick about you and then I saw you with that woman and . . ."

"And what, Dani?" he asked softly.

"And she was pawing you and I wanted to kill her." But then, he already knew that.

She trusted him. It had taken a few moments for that part to sink in, but Adam suddenly realized Dani had learned to trust. Grinning at the discovery, he filed away the speech he had intended to make about all the reasons Dani should trust him. It wasn't needed.

But something else was. "I suppose that means you would get into less trouble if I kept you briefed about what was going on?"

Dani grinned, sincerely hoping he was right. "Probably." Less trouble didn't mean no trouble, and she could tell he was regretting the way he had phrased the offer. She tried to reassure him. "I've already promised I won't interfere. Now I'll just have a better idea what I'm not interfering with!" she said, pleased with the logic behind her statement.

Adam didn't buy it, but then, he hadn't expected to. Dani was Dani, and there was no way he'd ever be able to change her. For that matter, he didn't want to.

"What made you think you could get away with it?" he asked, returning to current events. It made sense that anyone else would be slightly put off with a technique that had twice resulted in failure. Evidently, Dani wasn't intimidated by the occasional bomb.

"Third time's a charm?" Dani said, testing for his reaction.

"Do you think you'll give up on that particular scenario now?" Adam certainly didn't want her to get them banned from every restaurant in town. He enjoyed eating out.

"Do you think it's hopeless?" she asked seriously. She valued Adam's professional opinion on such things.

Adam shook his head in amused disbelief. She'd never give up. It was time to move on to other, more interesting subjects.

Putting his arm around her, he pulled her close, acutely aware of the softness of her breasts as they rested against his chest. He could even feel her pebble-hard nipples beneath the layers of clothing. Taking a deep breath, he struggled to say the words he'd been planning for what seemed an eternity. "We're getting married Saturday."

"Why?"

"Why Saturday?" he asked. "Because that's the soonest we can get the license."

"I meant 'Why are we getting married,' not 'Why Saturday.'" Dani decided that if she could say the words, then Adam was capable of the same thing.

He looked at her curiously, almost as if he doubted she was serious. Didn't she know how much he wanted her, needed her, loved her? "Because I love you and I want to marry you."

Her heart did flip-flops, not because she was surprised, but because she had needed to hear the words. He loved her. Her world was complete. Composing herself, she decided it was time to get even for the martini.

"No." Dani laid her head back on his supporting arm so she could watch his face. And, just as she'd predicted, his features contorted into an expression of disbelief.

"No?" Adam felt the world spinning away, out of control. She'd said no, she wouldn't marry him. But he pulled himself together long enough to notice the calculating watchfulness on Dani's face. She was doing it again, he groaned silently. When would he learn to look beyond her words to her meaning?

"No," she repeated. "Not on Saturday."

"Why not?"

"Because we're going to Las Vegas tonight."

He grinned. She had great ideas. But he had his own input on the decision. Sliding his hand around until he found the top of her zipper, he added, "Later tonight." His lips found the sensitive hollow behind her ear as he began to describe in graphic detail what they'd be doing in the meantime.

Dani shivered as the sapphire blue dress opened beneath his gentle touch. Yes, later was a good plan.

Evidently, the caller at the other end of the ringing telephone agreed.

With a reluctant sigh, Dani backed away from the heat of Adam's caress and picked up the offending instrument.

"I've finished reading the book. It's terrific."

Dani grinned. It was nice to have immediate feedback, even if it *did* come at a very inopportune moment. Flashing Adam a silent promise of an early return to his waiting arms, she took the opportunity to share her own news. "I'm getting married," she announced, delighted that Agnes was the first to hear the news.

"'I'm getting married' as in you and Adam?"

"Yes." Dani warmed under Adam's approving gaze. Sharing the news was another pledge, an added means to seal their promise to each other.

"That's terrific, too. May I come to the wedding?"

"It's tonight. In Las Vegas."

"See you there." Agnes didn't believe in wasting time—especially when there was none to spare.

Dani swore she'd call back as soon as the arrangements for transportation had been made and replaced the receiver. Moving back toward the exciting heat of Adam's open arms, she was startled once again by the telephone.

"You should unplug that thing," Adam suggested, not a little disenchanted with the miracle of communication.

"You threatened dire consequences the next time I did that," Dani reminded him as she halted mid-flight and returned to hush the demanding noise.

Adam only smiled, then grinned as he figured out the caller was Dani's mother.

"We're almost on our way to Las Vegas," Dani said in response to her mother's question. "Is that soon enough for you?"

"You're being precipitous, Dani," her mother responded with aplomb. "I'll hardly have time to call your brothers in that time, much less arrange to meet you there. Better you should make another plan."

"I'm not sure he'll wait," Dani replied with a grin in Adam's direction. "He seems very determined."

"Let me speak to Adam, Dani," her mother calmly replied. "I'm sure we can work something out."

Without a word, Dani handed the instrument to Adam, then used her idle fingers to work at the buttons on his shirt. That was much more interesting than holding a telephone, especially when she could allow herself to touch what the shirt concealed.

And when he trembled, Dani did the same. But *she* didn't have to worry about keeping her voice steady. Adam, on the other hand, was hanging onto his sanity with the barest thread.

"Tomorrow would be, er, fine." He stammered a little, flinching as Dani ran a fingernail across his very sensitive nipple. He tried to pay attention, but the distraction was incredibly strong. "We'll, uh, er, call in the morning. You make plans for yourselves, and we'll work around them." A pause, then he said, "Yes, Agnes will be coming with us." Another pause. "No, my folks are on vacation. We'll just have to do something later with them."

Dani had reached the last button, then hesitated only a second before attacking the belt buckle that guarded the other half of his torso. Apparently Adam could stand no more of this passive acceptance, because Dani heard him mumble a promise to call at first light before he rattled the phone onto its rest.

And she was prepared for the hands that stripped away her dress and flimsy underthings. Prepared, but certainly not immune to.

Adam wasted no time. He was hot, excited and ready.

Dani accepted the flame of his passion with a fervor that equaled that of the man she loved.

"WHEN ARE YOU going to tell me about that vagrancy charge?"

Dani stiffened in his arms. Dragging her eyes away from their rapturous study of the gold band that circled the third finger on her left hand, she coyly looked up into the mischievous eyes of her husband. Vagrancy charge, she silently repeated. He knew about her rap sheet.

"Well, love?" Adam waited for her answer, not nearly as interested in what she would say as he was in the creamy breast he cupped gently in one hand.

And if he knew about her rap sheet, he also knew about all the other charges that had been filed against her at one time or another. Yet he had still married her. Dani gasped as his fingers sought her already puckered nipple, desperately racking her brain for something extraordinary to say that would divert his attention from his question.

If Adam ever found out the truth behind the vagrancy charge, he'd never let her live it down. Last summer, Dani had dreamed up a complicated murder scenario involving an itinerant vagrant and a local businessman. Her research took her down near the tracks where transients lived in makeshift hovels and boxes. Not only had she failed to come up with any brilliant ideas for her book, but she'd also been caught up in a routine police sweep that was designed to inhibit vagrants from setting up permanent housekeeping. Not having brought any cash or identification, Dani had spent the night in jail before Agnes had been able to spring her.

No, she certainly couldn't tell Adam that story. Besides, with his fingers working their magic on her body, it was hard to do any proper thinking.

"Would you believe . . ." she started, then caught her breath as Adam lowered his lips to torment the nipple his fingers had brought to complete hardness.

"Probably not," he whispered, then moved quickly to cover her mouth with his own before she could say another word. Pushing his tongue deep inside her welcoming sweetness, he blessed the sudden intuition that had made him realize he really *didn't* want to know the truth.

But it wouldn't hurt to keep her guessing about when he'd remember to ask again.

Harlequin Temptation dares to be different!

Once in a while, we Temptation editors spot a romance that's truly innovative. To make sure *you* don't miss any one of these outstanding selections, we'll mark them for you.

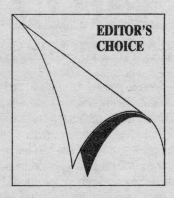

When the ''Editors' Choice'' fold-back appears on a Temptation cover, you'll know we've found that extra-special page-turner!

THE

Temptation

EDITORS

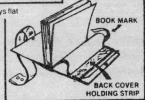

They went in through the terrace door. The house was dark, most of the servants were down at the circus, and only Nelbert's hired security guards were in sight. It was child's play for Blackheart to move past them, the work of two seconds to go through the solid lock on the terrace door. And then they were creeping through the darkened house, up the long curving stairs, Ferris fully as noiseless as the more experienced Blackheart.

They stopped on the second floor landing. "What if they have guns?" Ferris mouthed silently.

Blackheart shrugged. "Then duck."

"How reassuring," she responded. Footsteps directly above them signaled that the thieves were on the move, and so should they be.

For more romance, suspense and adventure, read Harlequin Intrigue. Two exciting titles each month, available wherever Harlequin Books are sold.